Nita's Treasure

The Hungry Gomulus

Jorge García Garrido

PUBLISHED BY JORGE GARCIA GARRIDO
Book title: *Nita's Treasure. The Hungry Gomulus*
Original title: *El tesoro de Nita: El no dragón hambriento*
Jorge García Garrido

Editor: Jorge García Garrido
Cover design: Jose Mari Morcillo Borrega
Layout: Jorge García Garrido
Translation: Molly Bechert

Published in Spain by Jorge García Garrido
ISBN **978-84-617-8122-5**

http://www.eltesorodenita.es

To my wife and my family.

JGG

CONTENTS

ACKNOWLEDGEMENTS

Thank you to Luis Haranburu, Patricia Del Olmo and Molly Bechert for their advice. And a special thanks to Joxemari for dedicating so much time and energy to this book.

1 FIRE WATER

Nita was a happy eleven-year-old girl with a huge imagination. She had a very pretty, kind face that would transform with an impish grin when she was about to get into some sort of mischief, which was often. Her real name was Elena, but Ángela, her grandmother, had started calling her Nita very soon after she was born. She loved her name. Her days were spent playing with her two best friends, Jaime and Amaya. They would often play traditional games, but Nita had a special talent for coming up with fun adventures for the three friends to go on. Amaya didn't have Nita's imagination, but she made up for it with her boundless enthusiasm. The two playmates complemented each other perfectly. They both had dark, straight hair, and looked very much alike. Some people could only tell them apart by the way they wore their hair. Jaime was the quietest of the three. He was as wide as the two girls put together and a head and a half taller than them.

1

No matter what they were playing, they always had fun together. That summer, time was flying by for the three friends. They lived in a time not too long ago, but technology was nowhere near as big a presence in people's lives as it is today. People had to use their imaginations to have fun and avoid falling prey to boredom. Nita and her friends were experts at that.

Hours and hours spent under the sun had turned Nita's white skin golden brown. The brown-eyed girl was playing with her two friends on the promenade by the harbor in her small town. She loved living in Pasai San Pedro, a small fishing town in northern Spain. She could see the harbor from her window, watch sea creatures made of wood and steel as they left to fish and then came back to rest at the docks. And if she looked beyond the parade of boats she could see the beautiful town of Pasai Donibane. Visiting the neighboring town was like going back in time. The streets, which were hundreds of years old, were paved in bumpy cobblestones worn down by centuries of use. Most of her time was spent playing on the promenade that ran along the harbor, accompanied by the sea breeze and the smell of salt water. The three friends would often end their days with a refreshing swim in the harbor.

Mount Ulía stood guard over the town. Besides the town of Pasai San Pedro, the mountain was also surrounded by the Bay of Biscay and the city of San Sebastián. Nita's grandmother had told her lots of stories about a good witch who lived on Mount Ulía. Now Nita lived with her mother, Adela, and Adela's boyfriend, José. Since her grandmother's death, she hadn't heard any more stories about Ulía. She didn't remember her father, but the void that might have been left by his absence was filled by José, who was a wonderful father figure.

The three children were running and playing, none of them imagining the events that were about to change their lives. It all started that summer evening when Nita and her friends were playing in the dim light of the streetlamps that lined the seaside promenade. Nearby, a dark figure was watching them from the shadows. The old man was named Anttón. He had been shrouded in mystery from the day he arrived in town; people had been curious about him at first, but his strange lifestyle soon made him one of the town's least popular residents. Nobody knew where he lived. In fact, no one but the police were interested in him at all. The tense political atmosphere of the province and other parts of Spain meant that the police kept a close eye on people who aroused their suspicion by moving too often from town to town. Anttón's face was cracked and wrinkled. A number of prominent scars could be seen on his arms and neck, and the summer sun made them even more visible. He had difficulty speaking. It wasn't that he stuttered, but it was clear that some past injury had severely damaged his vocal cords.

Nita's mother had to call her for dinner three times before she and her friends finally stopped playing. The three children said goodbye quickly, suspecting that their parents would be angry with them. Nita's mother scolded her for being disobedient. And not only had she not come home when she was called, but her room was a mess as well. Nita blurted out an excuse, but challenging her mother's authority was the wrong move. This was a battle she couldn't win, and one with terrible consequences: she got sent to bed without dinner.

José sat silently at the dinner table as Adela reprimanded Nita. Adela was a very attractive woman in her late thirties, with a sense of style that was modern for the time. José, who was a year or two younger than Adela, also had a modern look, and an athletic build. They made an enviable couple. Despite their modern look, their parenting style was traditional, and they dealt with the same parent-child power struggle found in all families.

The family's bedrooms were on the second floor of the house, and the first floor, which was at street-level, was where the family spent most of their time. Nita's bedroom was large and very simply decorated. There were a few stuffed animals arranged next to her school books on a shelf, and hanging on the wall next to the shelf was something very special: two terrifying African masks that she loved. José had brought them back for her from a recent trip to Africa. Sitting in her bed, Nita heard her stomach growl and was reminded of her fight with Adela, and then of the smell of the delicious meatloaf her mother had made in the small oven in their kitchen. Nita was intrigued by her mother's ability to make such delicious dishes using an appliance that was so mysterious to her and often subject to the inventions of her wild imagination. That was when she heard the noise. Floating through her window came the words, spoken in a deep, tortured voice and obscured by the grinding sound of metal gears and the creaking of wooden beams.

"I'm hungry," said the strange voice. "I'm hungry. She never came back."

Nita did what all children do when something scary invades the safest place in their lives, their beds: she curled up and pulled the covers over her head. Isn't it curious that the worst monsters tend to visit children in the dark and peaceful sanctuary of their bedrooms? Nita stayed under the covers for a moment before creeping up to the window to look outside: she decided she would be safely hidden in the shadows next to the window. She put her little face up against the glass to look out the window. She didn't see anyone in front of the house, or on the promenade, or—suddenly the window swung open. There was no crash or bang. The two doors of the window simply swung open slowly without making a noise, but Nita heard a whistle in the distance, like the sound the wind makes when it blows through the trees, and when the whistle stopped suddenly, the window stopped too, mid-swing. Nita could hear her heart pounding, cutting through the terrible silence that suddenly filled the room, making the air around her unbearably stifling.

"I'm hungry!" This time the voice boomed through the whole room, as if someone, or something, were right next to her. The same metal screeches, the sound of wood creaking, but she couldn't see anything. Nita moved away from the window and into the center of the room, looking all around her for the owner of the voice, but she didn't see anything.

"She never came. I'm hungry!" said the strange voice again. This time the voice was so loud that it knocked Nita over. She landed on the floor in front of the open window. An enormous head slowly emerged from the shadows. Nita's first thought was that the creature had to be incredibly large if he was able to look through her window, which was over fifteen feet above the ground. The only part of his face that she could see were two huge red eyes. A bright yellow light sparkled on the scales of his body. "I'm hungry," the beast said again. "I'm *hungry.*"

In an act of recklessness and naiveté, Nita slammed the window shut, trying to create a barrier between herself and the huge creature, although she knew the thin panes wouldn't protect her for long. "I'm hun—" began the beast again, before breaking off with a loud, rattling cough. After a moment, he finished: "—hungry." Then Nita watched as the giant creature moved away from the window and up the side of the house, all without touching the building; his body moved parallel to the house but never came into contact with the wall. It was as if the beast could manipulate gravity.

"What's the matter, Nita?" came her mother's voice from behind her. Nita jumped, startled. She had been so absorbed in what was outside her window that she hadn't heard her mother come in.

"You didn't see what was outside?" she asked her mother, her voice quick with fear. Adela, worried, looked out the window. Then she set down the dinner tray she was carrying on the bed.

"He was hungry! And somebody—" blurted an over-excited Nita.

"Come on, *txiki,*" her mother interrupted her, giving her a reassuring smile. "You had a long day, and you didn't have dinner. You'll feel better once you've had something to eat." Adela often called Nita *txiki,* the Basque word for "little one."

Nita looked out the window again. Reflected in the water, she saw a huge figure scaling the mountain behind their house. The reflection glittered beautifully, creating the illusion that there was a ball of fire on the water. It made Nita think of a sparkler.

"Have some dinner, Nita. It's getting cold," her mother urged again.

"You really didn't hear anything?" asked Nita, calmer now.

"It's just the wind blowing through these old walls. Sometimes you let your imagination get away from you," Adela said, shaking her head. "Your grandmother told you too many stories. Sometimes you remind me of h—" Her face froze and she stopped short, afraid of what she had been about to say. The similarities between Nita and her grandmother were undeniable, and the old woman's final years had been so terrible. "Finish your dinner and then bring the tray down." She kissed her daughter on the cheek and left the room.

After her mother left the room, Nita looked at the door, remembering how her grandmother used to tell her incredible stories before her "mental illness." That was what her mother called it. Nita still didn't understand what had been wrong with her; all she knew was that her grandmother had been a completely different person in the last two years of her life. But the truth was she didn't remember much about her father's disappearance or the years leading up to her grandmother's death.

She looked out the window again and suddenly felt excited. The fear she had felt ten minutes before had waned, and she was filled with intense curiosity. As she thought of the strange creature that appeared to be living in her town, and how she was going to trap it, a huge grin spread across her face, and it stayed there even as she stuffed her mouth full of food.

2 FEED ME

Nita got up very early the next morning after tossing and turning all night. Her encounter with the huge beast had her all wound up. She couldn't wait to trap the amazing creature. Her excitement had now completely eclipsed the fear she had felt at first. She picked up her room and put her dirty clothes in the wash. She needed her plan to go off without a hitch, and she knew that her mother was still angry with her for getting home late the day before. Adela had clearly won yesterday's battle, but Nita knew that a well-timed offensive move could work in her favor. She loved her mother very much and she was old enough to understand that disobeying the rules had consequences, but it was summertime. Her whole life was outside: her friends, the water, their games . . . was there anything more important?

"Nita, time for breakfast!" shouted Adela without looking up from the table, where she had laid out freshly squeezed orange juice, toast, jam and a cup of hot chocolate.

"It looks great, *Ama!*" said Nita with enthusiasm, as always using the Basque word for "mother." Adela jumped, surprised to find her daughter already at the table, since she had expected to have to call up to her at least a few more times to get her to come down for breakfast.

"Good morning. You're up early," she said as Nita tucked in to the breakfast. "Did you sleep all right last night, after everything?"

"Yes, mostly," said Nita, spreading jam on a piece of toast.

Adela studied her daughter, a worried look on her face, as dark, murky memories pushed their way to the front of her mind. She didn't want her beautiful daughter to suffer like her grandmother had. Adela's mother had been a lovely person, and, despite occasional clashes with her daughter over the strange stories she insisted on telling, she had been very happy. Until the last two years of her life. They were two years of sheer agony. Her mind had been so sharp her whole life, but in those last years it just shut down, went dark. In the end she couldn't remember anything at all, and then one day her heart just forgot to keep beating. She had lived a long life, and Adela didn't really believe anything like that would happen to Nita. Certainly not in the near future. But last night her mind had filled with images and words from her mother's final years, when the woman's mind had so cruelly abandoned her. Ángela had sacrificed so much for her family, and in the end something none of them could control left her with absolutely nothing.

After her big breakfast, Nita hurried into the living room, where she took out a piece of paper and began to draw what she had seen the night before. She hadn't seen the beast's whole body, but she had a big enough imagination to fill in the missing pieces. As she drew, the creature took shape, becoming a sort of wingless dragon with a dinosaur's body, covered in yellow scales. Adela looked over her daughter's shoulder at her picture and smiled, allowing herself to relax a little when she saw that Nita was drawing a dragon, a common subject in drawings by children her age. Things were back to normal.

"Nita! Nitaaaaa!" shouted Amaya from outside Nita's house.

When she heard her friend, Nita grabbed a small backpack and filled it with her picture of the beast, a bottle of water and some chips and candy she had left over from the day before. She ran to the door. "Nita, where do you think you're going? Did you clean your room?" Nita was itching to embark on the adventure she had planned for the day, but Adela's question stopped her in her tracks: it was time to resolve the power struggle that had begun the night before.

"I picked everything up *and* I put my dirty clothes in the wash." Nita's one-two punch had its intended effect on Adela, who raised her eyebrows in surprise. She suddenly understood why her daughter had been so unusually well-behaved that morning, but she was pleased that she had done what she had been asked, and she could see no reason not to let her go play.

"Remember, lunch is at two o'clock," she said to Nita, who was looking at her expectantly.

"See you later, Ama!" And with a huge grin on her face, Nita ran out the door.

Adela stared at the door after it closed behind her daughter. She was suddenly overwhelmed by a strange feeling. She didn't know what to call it, good or bad. She had had the same feeling a few times before, always right before some important moment in her life: she had felt it when she met José, when Nita's father disappeared, when her mother got sick. That morning, there were signs that her daughter was up to something—there was the fact that she had taken her backpack with her, the drawing of the strange creature—but Adela had failed to see their significance. If she had paid attention to the signs and allowed herself to trust her premonition, she may have kept her daughter from setting in motion the life-changing events that would take place in the next few days. But she brushed the feeling aside. Just as she always had, she decided that it was just a physical reaction to something going on in her life; this time it was probably her worries about Nita. Life had put her to the test more than once, and her whole body had reacted every time. She felt the import of these moments like an electric current buzzing back and forth between somewhere deep within her gut to the tiniest hairs on the outermost layer of her skin. But she didn't let herself consider the possibility that she had a gift, that she could sense the future: it was pure chemistry, she told herself, nothing more.

Nita ran to meet Amaya and Jaime, who were each clutching a piece of thick rope. The day before they had agreed that they would play jump rope today. Tall, heavyset Jaime wasn't exactly enthusiastic about the idea, because it was thought of as a girls' game, but he had brought a rope anyway because he knew that with Nita and Amaya, the day could always take an unexpected turn and they could end up doing something else. Anyway, even if they did play jump rope for a while, they would probably get to go for a swim in the harbor afterwards. Jaime was kind and even-tempered. He was scared of lots of things, but he wasn't a coward.

Nita had completely forgotten that they had planned to play jump rope that morning. She showed her friends her drawing and told them about the strange beast that had come to visit her the night before. She told the whole story so enthusiastically that her enthralled audience even let out a gasp or two when she got to the scary parts.

"Are you sure it wasn't just gas?" asked Jaime, his eyes wide. "Sometimes when I'm hungry my stomach growls so much it sounds like someone's voice," he suggested gently. Jaime loved Nita and the games she made up, so he didn't want to cast doubt on her story, but the thought of a huge beast on the loose in his town made him very nervous.

"It was an animal!" insisted Nita, annoyed. "I'm not a liar! Why would I lie to you guys?"

"And it couldn't have been an owl or something?" asked a very skeptical Amaya. She didn't know a lot about animals, but she had seen a few owls at the winter fair held in the nearby city of San Sebastián on Saint Thomas Day last year, and she had been very impressed with their enormous eyes and huge wings.

"No!" insisted Nita, and with a resigned look she told them the last part of the story, when she saw the beast climb up Mount Ulía, the mountain behind her house. Nita was sure they would find the strange animal there, and her friends would see that she was telling the truth.

It took some convincing, but Nita was a very persuasive person, and soon the three friends set out to climb the mountain. It wasn't their first time climbing Mount Ulía, which had a wealth of interesting spots to explore. And at certain times of year, usually in the fall, entire families would often hike up the mountain to collect chestnuts, hazelnuts and pinecones. They looked like hunter-gatherers from an ancient society. The climb up was a little steep, but it was short, and after a relatively brief climb, the mountain opened up into patches of woods full of trees, crisscrossed by different paths. The north face of the mountain dropped off abruptly where it met the sea, forming very steep cliffs. The paths around the cliffs offered beautiful views of the expansive Bay of Biscay, whose angry waters were unrelenting in their determination to swallow the mountain bit by bit, pounding the rock in constant, almost rhythmic waves. Those narrow paths were dangerous, and the children knew to stay away from them. Even though they were very familiar with the mountain, they weren't allowed to go there by themselves, but these were simpler times, and parents weren't as protective of their children as they are today. For better or for worse, this allowed young people a certain degree of freedom that today's children don't have.

Amaya and Jaime put their ropes in Nita's backpack, their game of jump rope postponed, and the three children began to hike up the mountain. As they climbed, Jaime looked around nervously. He was a head and a half taller than his two friends, but he wasn't the bravest of the three. He wasn't a coward, either, as he had proved when he stood up to two boys from school who were picking on Amaya. Amaya and Jaime had been inseparable since that day, and they had discovered Nita together in almost the same way. The same boys, whose idea of a good time involved picking on their classmates, had shoved the little girl back and forth between them until Nita grabbed a stick from the ground and dealt the boys two very well-placed blows. Jaime and Amaya witnessed the encounter in amazement. They were running over to help her when they saw both bullies double over in pain, and suddenly Nita was coming toward them at full speed. Amaya and Jaime turned on their heels and they all ran in the same direction, not knowing exactly where they were going, until they finally came to a stop in an alley. The three children looked at each other and burst out laughing. They knew each other from school before that, but from that moment on, they were best friends.

Amaya was following Nita along the path, but she suddenly stopped short, her eyes going wide with a sudden realization. "Wait a second!" she demanded, and Nita and Jaime stopped in their tracks. "How exactly are we supposed to find this thing?" Nita narrowed her eyes thoughtfully, but she had an answer ready: she had had lots of time to think of a plan last night.

"I brought food," she replied. "He's really hungry. We're going to put the food out and hide, and we'll see him when he comes out to eat."

"What if he doesn't like your food? What if he'd rather eat"—Jaime gulped before continuing—"humans?"

"Don't be such scaredy-cats," Nita said firmly. "Have you heard of anyone getting eaten on Mount Ulía lately? Or kids disappearing?"

Jaime looked at her, wide-eyed. Nita's questions, far from quelling his fears, brought horrifying images into his head.

"No," said Amaya calmly. "But nobody's going to believe us. Did you bring a camera?"

Nita looked at her thoughtfully. She was right. Why hadn't she thought of that? She could have taken the Polaroid camera José had given her mother.

"Damn," she said, angry with herself.

Jaime regarded his friend nervously. He had a solution to the problem but he was scared to suggest it because it was risky, and he didn't like taking risks.

"I think I can—" he began, cutting off when Nita and Amaya both turned to look at him at once. "I can use the ropes to make a trap."

"Yes!" shouted Nita. She ran to Jaime and threw her arms around him. Jaime turned red, enjoying the close contact with his pretty friend. "Do you really think you could make one?" she asked, stepping back to look at him.

Jaime nodded. He loved reading books on hunting, and he knew a lot of different ways to catch animals. His father was an expert hunter; he had told Jaime tons of hunting stories and tricks. None of the children thought about what they would do with the animal after they caught it, or whether the beast would suffer, or whether the trap would even work given the immense strength that a creature of the size Nita had described would presumably have. When they set out again they didn't notice that someone was following them through the trees.

The three friends stopped at the point in the path where Nita guessed they were right above her house. They started looking for signs that a very large animal had passed through the area recently. When they didn't find anything, they decided to venture further inward, and eventually reached a wooded area with a path covered in leaves running through it. Something caught Jaime's eye. The blanket of leaves was uniform except for a spot where it looked like someone had dragged a rake across the path, clearing two lines that were about two feet wide and six feet apart. The three young hunters examined the area around the marks on the ground, but they didn't find any footprints. They continued farther down the path and found more lines cutting across the leaves.

Nita examined the trees that lined the trail, looking for more signs of the beast in the vegetation. And then she saw them: there was a dense growth of hazel trees that made it difficult to enter the woods, and lying on the ground in front of the trees were a number of small, shiny yellow stones. She noticed that a few of the trees had scratch marks on them. In Nita's small hand all the small yellow stones looked nearly identical. They reminded her of shells, but they were incredibly light. The children examined them and concluded that they were scales. If the scales had belonged to a fish, the animal would have been the size of a large whale.

Amaya enjoyed listening to her friends' theories, but she didn't think they were scales. They looked like dry yellow leaves to her. They must have come from one of the trees or bushes in the woods. But the game was fun anyway, and she happily joined in with Jaime and Nita as they searched for more. They had their hands full of scales—or leaves—when a gust of warm air suddenly blew in, disintegrating everything they had picked up and the rest of the evidence that remained on the ground. The children watched in amazement as a wisp of yellow smoke faded into the air.

"They just disappeared," said a puzzled Nita. "We should set the trap here." Amaya smiled at her friends, still enjoying the game, but the leaves had probably disintegrated like that because they were so dry.

Jaime found a tree that was tall and flexible enough to provide the tension he would need to set a snare that could catch an animal the size of a German shepherd. The children armed themselves with big sticks from a hazel tree and hid behind some bushes. For bait, they used some fried cheese balls with a strong smell, which were very popular among children in those days. Nita had some left over from the day before. Jaime added half of the chocolate bar he had brought.

Nita yawned. The excitement of the night before and the hike up the mountain were beginning to catch up to her. She nestled comfortably between her two friends and began to bob her head sleepily. Finally, she dozed off, her chin on her chest.

Suddenly the sound of branches breaking startled her from sleep. She was alone in their hiding spot, and a thick fog covered everything. She scrambled to her feet nervously and saw a woman dressed in a sleeveless white dress kneeling where the trap should have been, plucking a small branch from the ground. She looked familiar; something about her reminded Nita of her mother. Nita approached her, gripping her hazel stick tightly. The woman in white smiled at her and held out her arm, her hand closed around something. When she opened her hand Nita saw that she was holding a silver bracelet with a charm on it. It was shaped like a tree branch with some sort of lizard wrapped around it. With the small branch she held in her other hand the woman began to draw circles in the air, and a ring of smoke appeared. But unlike cigarette smoke rings, this one didn't fade. Instead it became more solid by the second.

Suddenly from the thick fog to Nita's left came the sound of a huge creature breathing in and out. She couldn't get a good look at the beast through the fog, but she could see the outline of its enormous body. Nita looked back at the beautiful woman and saw that she was smiling kindly, but a noise coming from the fog drew the little girl's attention away again. The jaws of an enormous animal emerged from the heavy mist and loomed over the defenseless Nita.

"Nita!" shouted Jaime, waking her from her incredible dream. "You were screaming in your sleep."

"Did the animal come?" asked Nita sleepily.

"No, all we saw were a couple of little birds who flew off

with some cheese balls," answered Amaya, who was starting to get bored.

"We should get back," said Jaime. He didn't want to be late for lunch.

The three patient hunters left their hiding place and approached the trap, discussing what to do with it. Jaime and Amaya wanted their ropes back, but Nita thought they should leave the snare set and come back in the afternoon. Jaime and Amaya won the argument in the end and were just about to undo the trap when a gust of warm air swept the leaves off the ground and enveloped the children in a cloud of debris. The leaves, dirt and sticks flying around the children trembled unnaturally in the air. They seemed to be levitating. Nita and Jaime, wide-eyed, looked up at the sky and saw a huge figure flying toward them at full speed. When it looked like it was going to crash into the ground, it stopped in the air and hovered just above the path. Nita and Jaime watched the huge beast, frozen in shock.

Amaya looked all around in confusion. She didn't see what her friends were seeing. Yes, the air felt a little different, and there were leaves blowing around, but she couldn't see what Jaime and Nita were looking at. "Weren't we leaving?" she shouted. She didn't understand why her friends weren't moving.

Jaime couldn't take his eyes off the beast's huge mouth. He had a set of artificial teeth made of branches, bits of tree trunk and metal gears. An enormous scar cut across the animal's impressive face, running from his mouth to the top of his head and passing through his right eye, which was cloudy. His face was adorned with piercings that had chains hanging from them, his body covered in yellow scales that glittered in the sunlight like huge sequins. There were chains hanging from metal rings incrusted in his sides. They looked like they had been placed there for a rider. The beast was the size of the largest known mastodon, more than fifteen feet tall and twenty-five feet long. Each limb had five fingers that ended in heavy claws. Some of the claws were broken, others full of small cracks and notches. The beast had a large fin on his back, extending from the top of his head to the end of his large tail, and a membrane that ran the length of the underside of his body, ending at his chin. His tail had a large fan that he could open and close. The animal's skeleton was incredibly light and had internal cavities, so he could use his tail fan and the membranes that ran along his body to hover in the air without touching the ground, like a huge fish floating in the water, the membranes on his body constantly waving in the air.

"I'm hungry!" the beast said to the three children. "If you don't feed me, I'll gobble you up!"

Nita noticed that the beast had a number of earrings hanging from his right ear. Among them was the bracelet that the strange woman in white had held out to her in her dream. Nita suddenly felt an urge to take it. The beast's snout was only feet away from her, and she thought that if she ran, she could easily pull the earring off. But first she would have to overcome the fear that was paralyzing her, and then attempt the impossible: avoid ending up in the monster's jaws.

"You look plump and tasty," said the strange animal, sniffing Jaime. Suddenly, as if by instinct, he turned to Nita, who jumped back in fear. "You . . . you smell like her . . ." said the creature. The beast's voice softened then. "I'm hungry," he said meekly. "Feed me," he implored. "Give me something to eat."

"Are we leaving or aren't we?" asked Amaya angrily, moving to stand in front of Nita and Jaime, who were still too scared to move. Amaya couldn't see or hear anyone, only her friends.

"I'll gobble you all up!" shouted the beast as he drew back in fear, pulling back his front legs as if touching Amaya would have deadly consequences. Like his reaction to Nita, this seemed to be instinctive. Jaime took a step back, forgetting the snare that he had so carefully set earlier. The rope closed on his legs and suddenly he was hanging upside down in the air. He was so terrified he couldn't even scream. The beast, startled, lurched forward. Nita threw herself on Amaya to push her out of the path of the enormous creature. The two girls got to their feet quickly and they both spun around to look at their friend. Amaya didn't understand what was going on.

"Hey, that hurt!" cried Amaya.

Nita thrust Amaya's stick into her hands and grabbed her own before running off to face the beast.

"He's going to eat me!" cried a terrified Jaime as the monster pounced on him, grabbing him with his left front claws. He braced himself, expecting his bones to break like twigs in such a powerful hand.

"Untie the rope, Mayi!" Nita shouted, calling Amaya by her nickname. Amaya saw Jaime swinging upside down, but she didn't understand why her friends seemed so scared. He actually looked pretty funny to her. But she ran to the rope anyway, remembering that Jaime had tied a simple knot that would be very easy to untie.

Rushing to help her friends, Nita suddenly saw a clear path that would allow her to easily climb up onto the giant beast. She launched herself off the ground, grabbed onto one chain and used another to support her feet. She climbed up to the animal's shoulder, but her stick slipped from her fingers on the way. Without hesitating, she grabbed at the beast's right ear, the one that was full of huge earrings, and punched him in the right eye. The animal, more startled than hurt, shook Nita off, sending her flying in the air with the charm bracelet clenched in her fist.

Amaya had untied the rope holding the trap by then, and Jaime fell to the ground just as Nita was punching the huge beast. Amaya and Jaime watched powerlessly from the ground as their dear friend began to fall from a height of nearly fifteen feet. There was nothing to break her fall, and she was going to land on her back. They held their breath. When she was about to hit the ground, the beast flicked his tail at her, giving her a push that sent her rolling gently onto the path.

"Run!" she shouted to her friends from the ground. They all scrambled to their feet and, although they were tired and bruised, they began to run, fueled by adrenaline and by the terrifying sensation that they could be gobbled up at any minute. They didn't look back, and they didn't stop until they reached the harbor near Nita's house.

"What was that, Nita?" shouted Jaime, who was panting from exertion.

"What was what?" Amaya asked, her face reflecting her confusion. She hadn't seen anything.

"You didn't see the monster?" asked Jaime, now even more confused than Amaya was.

"What monster?" She hadn't seen anything out of the ordinary, except for Nita's fall, which she couldn't really explain.

"There was a monster with huge teeth and chains and scales and"—he gulped in air—"he was going to eat us!"

The three friends looked at each other uneasily. They agreed that they would tell their families what they had seen, leaving out the part where they went up the mountain by themselves. Then they all ran home. Amaya wouldn't say anything to her parents, since she didn't really understand what had happened. Jaime promised that he would talk to his father, but the idea of going back up the mountain to hunt the beast didn't appeal to him at all. Nita was convinced that they had to tell their parents what they had seen, or someone could get hurt.

3 THE KEY OF DESTINY

Nita burst through the door, still buzzing with adrenaline from what they had seen on Mount Ulía, without giving a thought to what she looked like. Her overalls were covered in dirt from rolling on the ground after falling from the shoulder of the huge beast. She was clutching the earring she had ripped from the animal's ear. Up close, she had seen that his ear was covered in scars from an encounter with who knows what rival or monster, and pierced by more than ten earrings. She looked at her mother and José, who were sitting at the table, about to eat lunch. She squeezed the earring in her hand—this was her proof that she wasn't just seeing things—and ran to the table.

"Ama, we just saw a huge monster!"

Adela looked at her daughter in surprise, taking in her dirty clothes. "Nita, you're filthy! What on earth have you been up to?" As her mother spoke, Nita had a sudden revelation: no one was going to believe her. She was just a little girl.

"Can't you find something to play that doesn't involve

rolling around in the dirt?" her mother continued, getting up angrily from the table.

"But Ama, didn't you hear me? We saw this huge creature! He's hiding on Mount Ulía!"

Adela stood in front of her daughter and looked at her disapprovingly. "You went up Ulía by yourselves?"

Nita looked down. She didn't want to lie to her mother. "Ama, he could attack someone! We have to call the police!"

Her mother looked at her, worry and anger written on her face, then took her by the arm and pulled her toward the stairs that led to their bedrooms. "We're going to change your clothes before you get dirt all over the house. And stop talking nonsense!" She tugged Nita's arm angrily as they went up to her room.

José watched them leave in silence, his face serious. He was intrigued by Nita's story. After a few seconds he began to eat.

Adela seemed angrier than normal as she struggled to pull her daughter's dirty clothes off. "Monsters, creatures . . . it's just crazy," she muttered under her breath.

Her reaction was making Nita just as angry as she was. It wasn't the first time she had gotten her clothes a little dirty, and her mother had never reacted this way. "I'm not making it up! We saw a huge"—she stopped to think, trying to find the best word to describe it—"a huge yellow dragon!" She stood there in her underwear, waiting for her mother to say something. "It had these things that looked like fins, and it could fly, and—"

"Jesus, Elena!" When Adela called her by her full name and gave her the look she was giving her right now, it was best not to argue. But although she hated to fight with her mother, Nita couldn't stop thinking about what had happened.

"I pulled an earring off his ear," she said with a sigh, and, more calmly now, held the earring out to her mother. Adela stopped rooting through her daughter's drawers, where she was looking for an outfit for her so they could get on with eating lunch, and glanced at the bracelet. She gasped.

"Where did you get that?" she asked, bewildered.

"I took it from the monster," repeated Nita nervously.

Adela took the bracelet from her daughter and examined it. "This is your grandmother's silver bracelet," she said, touching the small charm that hung from the chain.

"Can I see?" said Nita, moving to take it back from her mother. Adela held on to it for a few more seconds before giving the little treasure back to her daughter. Nita looked at it closely, surprised and excited to find that it hadn't broken like she had thought, but had opened at the clasp. It looked like the bracelet had somehow come undone by itself, because it had a barrel clasp with two ends that had to be screwed together. Or maybe it had been hanging unclasped from the beast's ear.

Adela took a short-sleeved shirt and a pair of jeans out of the wardrobe. "Put this on and come down to eat. Lunch is getting cold." She took one last look at her daughter, who was still entranced by the treasure in her hands, before leaving the room. As she walked through the doorway, she felt a chill run down her back. Memories of her mother began to rush through her head, forcing her to relive some of the worst moments of her life: her mother's dementia and the disappearance of the love of her life, Nita's father, Raúl.

Adela walked into the kitchen, visibly upset. José took in her pale face and immediately knew something was wrong. "Are you okay, honey?" he asked her.

"Yeah, don't worry. I'm just cold all of the sudden."

Without hesitating, José got up from his chair and wrapped her in a hug. Adela let herself sink into his arms.

"Do you think she's making this up to get attention?" José's words brought Adela out of her brief moment of calm as she remembered Nita's story.

"She never lies. It's so strange," she answered thoughtfully, resting her head on José's chest.

"I have an idea. Why don't I take her up Ulía this afternoon? I'm sure she'll feel better once she sees there's nothing there," suggested José. He was happy to have the chance to do something to help the woman he loved, and it would also be a great opportunity to get closer to Nita, who was the coolest little girl he had ever met. He had been living with them for almost three years now, and he was head over heels in love with both of them. "I'm not trying to replace her father, but this is something I can do to help you two, and I want to—I *have to* do it."

Adela gazed into his eyes, overcome by the desire to kiss his beautiful lips and give in to a moment of intense pleasure, to forget lunch, and Nita's stories, and worrying about where on earth her soul mate, Nita's father, was. Then Nita came into the dining room, and the moment was over. The family sat down to a delicious lunch.

Nita and José were hiking up the mountain that she and her friends had barreled down just hours before with only one thought in their minds: getting away from the dangerous creature living on Mount Ulía and reaching the safe haven of their small town. Nita had insisted on calling the police, but José convinced her that it made more sense to check out the spot first. That way they would have more concrete information to bring to the police. The truth was José would rather keep the police out of his life.

As they hiked, José glanced at Nita and noticed that she was wearing a silver bracelet. The charm on it looked familiar, but he brushed the thought away. They discussed the characteristics of the beast as they walked. José was very amused by how passionately Nita told her story about what had happened to the three young hunters that morning. He made a show of scaring off any animals that might be around, picking up a thick branch and banging it hard against a tree next to the path. Nita jumped, startled by the force of the blow, even though she had been watching José. Then she grinned, thinking that it would be a good way to keep the beast at bay. There were a lot of farms in the area, and on a school field trip she had seen farmers get their cows to move by hitting them with sticks like the one José was holding. But her smile faded when she remembered that the beast they were looking for was no cow.

They arrived at the spot where the children had set the trap, but there was nothing there, not even crumbs from the bait they had left. Nita didn't understand. There was no trace of the huge animal either. Suddenly they heard a noise coming from behind some trees nearby. Nita and José approached the trees cautiously. Nita walked behind José, who was careful to put himself between her and whatever was in front of them, in case it turned out to be a dog or another wild animal. José struck the ground hard a few times with his stick, making a loud noise. A familiar old man stepped out from behind the trees and walked toward the path. Nita and José didn't see him toss the children's ropes on the ground behind him.

"I should have known you were behind this," said José with a familiarity that suggested he had known the old man for a long time.

"I didn't do anything," replied Anttón with great difficulty. The injury to his vocal cords made it very hard for him to talk, and what little voice he did have was raspy. His eyes landed on Nita's wrist and he looked at her in surprise. Nita was frightened and moved further behind José. "You shouldn't be here," croaked Anttón ominously.

"What do you mean, old man?" José answered rudely. "Who made you the king of the forest?" Anttón looked down nervously. "Hang on, was it you who scared the kids this morning?" José accused the old man, anger creeping into his voice. Anttón shook his head, denying his involvement in the strange events of that morning. "What did you do with that huge dog of yours?"

"Don't you dare talk about—" Anttón looked at José straight in the eye, defiant. The look had its intended effect, and José backed down. He turned to Nita, intending to reassure her. "Get as far away from him as you can!" Anttón said firmly, staring at Nita. Frightened, she took a step back.

"Stop scaring her with your nonsense!" spat José.

"You know I'm not trying to scare her. Why did you do it, you bastard?" Anttón stared at José and Nita, his face twisted in rage.

"What are you talking about, old man?" answered José. He gripped the stick tighter. "How dare you insult me—"

The huge beast suddenly emerged from the woods on the other side of the path and scooped Nita up in his mouth before taking off into the air. The rush of air from the flying beast made José lose his balance. He recovered just in time to see a huge blur rush past him. Anttón smiled as he watched the beast fly off with the girl in his jaws. For now, at least, everything was going according to plan. An astonished José sprinted off, trying desperately to keep his eyes on the figure in the air.

Half of Nita's body was inside the mouth of the huge beast and the other half was dangling from the side. She was wedged between two of the gears that made up the strange mechanism that seemed to control the animal's artificial teeth. It smelled like rust and wet wood. She braced herself for the immense pain she knew she would feel any minute now, from a broken bone or something much worse. She looked down: they were flying over Mount Ulía, past the mouth of the Pasaia River, and heading at full speed toward Mount Jaizkibel, tracing the curves of the rocky coast. They had flown past some of the many spots where the coast jutted out into the sea, when the creature suddenly began to gasp for air, and it lost control. The world spun around her as they plummeted toward the rocks. Nita's lunch was practically in her throat when they crashed into the rocks near Argorri Point. Everything went dark.

José burst into Adela's house, in anguish over what had happened on Mount Ulía. Adela already seemed to know that something had happened. She was in the kitchen, nervously nibbling at a snack.

"What's wrong?" she asked with a start.

"It's Nita! I don't even know what happened!" José answered quickly. "She stepped away for a second and then she was gone!"

For a moment, Adela stood frozen in front of José, thinking about the strange feelings she had had lately and how stupid she had been for not knowing how to read them. "We have to call the police!" she said finally, and ran to the phone they had in the kitchen.

A devastated José watched her, barely listening to her conversation with the police. Nita had been right behind him. And then there was a gust of warm air and something had taken her away. Suddenly he had a flash of Anttón's face. That stupid old man had to be involved in this whole thing somehow. His face was burned in his memory. He must know what had happened. But how was he going to get the information out of him?

"How can an eleven-year-old girl who's standing right next to you just disappear?" shouted Adela, her voice shaking with anguish and anger. She was on the verge of sobbing.

"Something just took her away . . ." answered José, looking away. Adela, crying now, grabbed her jacket from the back of a kitchen chair and ran outside. José watched his devastated girlfriend run out of the house. He felt so powerless, and at the same time a feeling of rage was coursing through his body. In that moment all he wanted to do was break something, destroy something. His body tense, he ran after Adela.

The town's residents sprung into action. They were all familiar with Mount Ulía, and because the mountain was relatively small, they were able to organize themselves into multiple search parties that would cover the different paths that cut across Ulía like scars, giving them access to the whole mountain. Adela joined the group that would be searching the path that ran along the cliffs. The path was treacherous, especially at night, and it was starting to get dark already. The cliffs were very high, and at the bottom lay jagged rocks that had been worn down by the sea. Now they were slowly being swallowed up by the water again as the tide came in.

Nita was jolted awake by the sound of a wave crashing against the rocks. A spray of salt water dampened her clothes and face. In front of her was the enormous head of the monster. She jumped back in fear and found herself with her back against a rocky wall. She looked up and saw that they were at the bottom of a cliff. An enormous wall loomed above her, making her very aware of the fact that she was trapped between the creature that had brought her there and a seemingly insurmountable wall. To make matters worse, the tide was rising. The huge animal appeared to be unconscious. Once in a while he heaved a shuddering breath. If she wanted to get out of there she would have to climb over him. She got up and took a step toward him.

"I'm hungry!" shouted the beast suddenly. "If you don't feed me I'm going to have to gobble you up"—he broke off suddenly with a cough. The creature struggled to his feet and faced the little girl. Nita, frightened, backed away.

"I don't have any food!" she shouted. She didn't understand what the beast expected her to do. His enormous head came closer.

"Then you leave me no other choice," said the beast. Nita, terrified, closed her eyes.

She braced herself for the unimaginable pain of being ripped apart by the beast, but it never came. Confused, she opened one eye to peek at him. The beast stepped away, whining.

"I can't take it anymore. My stomach hurts, my head hurts, my bones hurt," he whined, pacing back and forth on the rock they were standing on. Then he turned on Nita suddenly. "I haven't eaten in over a thousand days. I haven't slept." Nita looked at the beast in surprise.

"Why don't you eat grass, or wild animals?" she asked, overcome by curiosity.

"I don't like them, and they don't fill me up," the beast responded, looking at her. "She promised me she would feed me. She let me eat her food. But then she never came back. She disappeared," he finished, hanging his head.

"Who is this 'she'?" asked Nita, feeling bolder now.

"My keeper, my friend, my comrade in arms, my nourishment, my rest . . ." answered the beast, his voice heavy with nostalgia. Suddenly he spun around and brought his face close to Nita again, sniffing her. "You smell like her! You look like her!" Nita, startled, backed away again. Suddenly she remembered the woman in white from the dream she had had that morning. When the beast saw her step back in fear, his face clouded. He lowered his eyes and turned around.

"Are you a dragon?" ventured Nita.

"No, I'm not a dragon!" the beast shot back. "Those stupid winged lizards, with their foul breath . . ."

"What are you then?" she asked with interest.

"She used to call me Gom . . ." the beast replied sadly. "I am a gomulus, son of the wind and the clouds, the largest and strongest of all the gomuluses on this coast," he continued, his chest puffing with pride.

"I'm Nita," said the girl.

"I already know what you smell like and what you taste like. I don't need to know your name," said Gom.

"Take me home," begged Nita.

"I'm too weak to fly. I need to rest."

Nita watched as the huge gomulus lay down on the rock, just as a giant wave broke nearby. *The next one might sweep us away,* she thought. That's when Nita remembered how the woman in white from her dream had drawn a smoke ring in the air. Using her right hand, where she was wearing the bracelet, Nita began to draw circles like the woman had, and a ring of smoke appeared. Gom raised his head to look. Nita, startled by the movement, stopped moving her hand and the ring faded away.

"Yes, that's right . . ." said the beast excitedly. Nita, intrigued, kept her eyes on Gom while she began to move her hand in the air again, drawing three circles in the same spot until another smoke ring, this one denser than the first, appeared in the air in front of her. It floated there for a moment until the giant animal, who had been so weak just a moment ago, leapt up and gulped it down in one bite. "What is this delicacy?" he asked as he swallowed, chuckling with delight. Nita didn't know what to say. The huge animal stood there, waiting for an answer. What did he expect her to tell him? Nita cast around for something to say, and then she had an idea: "It's a giant anise-flavored doughnut," she said firmly. She had tried them with her mother at La Bretxa Market in San Sebastián and thought they were delicious.

Gom looked at her in surprise. "Yes, yes, you're right! *That's* what it is, an anise doughnut!" he laughed. The huge animal continued to chuckle, positively delighted with his meal. "Give me more!" he ordered Nita, who was amazed by what she was seeing. She made more doughnuts, each of which was gobbled up by the gomulus, who was becoming more excited by the minute.

Adela and José were on Mount Ulía. They were beside themselves with worry over Nita's disappearance, and they didn't know what to do. Night had fallen and they couldn't see anything in the dark, but they couldn't make themselves leave. Adela was resting her head on José's shoulder. She blamed herself for what had happened. She couldn't stop thinking about it: she shouldn't have let them go up the mountain. But the thought was absurd, she realized: how could she have known something would happen? All they had done was hike up a little mountain they had been up many times before; nothing should have gone wrong.

Anttón had been watching them through the trees. He walked up to them, startling them both.

"You, old man! You know where she is!" shouted José.

"Miss A . . . A—" began Anttón, but he stopped suddenly when he tried to say her name. "Don't worry. The girl will turn up," he croaked nervously.

Adela regarded the old man, surprised at how strangely familiar he looked. She felt reassured by his words, which also surprised her. She took a step toward him. "Do you know where my daughter is?" she asked with tears in her eyes.

Anttón looked away. Suddenly someone shouted from the woods, drawing their attention. Adela ran toward the noise, flashlight in hand. When she was out of earshot José turned to Anttón. "You shouldn't be here. You're not *allowed* to be here," he hissed at the old man. He held his gaze for a few seconds and then ran after Adela. Anttón watched them leave, his face grim.

Gom was in ecstasy, inhaling the smoky shapes that Nita was happily making for him. It was clear from the sheer joy Nita's creations gave him that the beast was wholly dependent on the smoke rings for nourishment. Nita drew a smoky "A" and told the hungry gomulus that she had made him fresh almonds. "Mmmm, what delicious almonds!" he exclaimed, his voice much stronger than it had been just moments before. She drew a huge "L" and told him it was lamb. The beast jumped for joy, scrambling up the near-vertical wall of the cliff and then back down again, head pointed toward the ground, like a four-ton lizard. He launched himself off the wall and landed on some nearby rocks, giggling in delight. "It's all delicious! I love it!" he exclaimed, before breaking off with a loud cough that forced his dentures out of his mouth and into the water. He dived in after them and, after putting them back in, gave Nita a beaming, grotesque grin that offered the fascinated girl a close look at the many gears and tree trunks that made up the strange mechanism. Then he lay down, resting his front legs on the rock where Nita was standing. Looking at her, he suddenly grew quiet. "I hadn't eaten in more than a thousand days . . . I hadn't slept. But I'm full now," he said, his face drooping with sleepiness.

It took him only a few seconds to fall asleep. Nita looked on contentedly as the beast fell asleep, until the sound of a wave breaking on the rocks interrupted her brief moment of peace and brought her back to reality, where she was in mortal danger for what seemed like the umpteenth time that day.

"Gom, wake up! You have to get me out of here!" she shouted, fear in her voice. All she could see was the beast's head and the rock closest to her. The darkness was broken only by the spray of the waves that crashed against the rocks every few seconds. The fierce waters of the Bay of Biscay were trying to swallow the mountain. Nita grabbed a pebble and threw it hard at Gom's head, but it bounced off with no effect on the huge beast. "The water's getting higher! We're going to drown!" she shouted, her voice louder now.

"Water is good . . . Mmmm," murmured Gom sleepily.

"Gom, wake up! I'm going to—" A wave knocked her off her feet and she fell backwards, screaming. As the wave receded, the water pulled her toward the ocean, but when she reached Gom's head she was able to grab onto a chain that ran from his nose to his cheek. "I can't hold on! I'm going to drown!" she screamed.

"You could always use the key," murmured Gom.

"What key?" she shouted desperately. Another wave broke over her and she felt herself pushed toward the rocky wall of the cliff, but she clung desperately to the chain. This time, at least, the ocean didn't succeed in claiming Nita. Then her eyes landed on the bracelet. The bracelet had to be the key Gom was talking about! The next wave hit harder than the last, wrenching her from the beast and picking her up ten feet in the air before throwing her against the wall of the cliff. Nita threw out her arms, finding a hold on the wall, and used all her strength to cling to the rock. The darkness had swallowed everything, even the beast below her. She moved her hand, searching for a crack in the rock that she could use to scale the wall. Suddenly her bracelet began to glow, emitting a soft light that warmed her entire arm. The light illuminated the rock in front of her, revealing a small hole. She moved her hand away from the hole and the light went out. Then she brought her hand close again and it glowed bright. She saw that the charm on the bracelet had changed shape, taking on the form and size of the hole. She heard a loud crash below, and suddenly the water was rushing up toward her. Nita grasped the charm and thrust it into the small hole in the wall of the cliff. And then the water swallowed everything. When the wave receded it revealed only hard rock. There was no trace of the girl.

Nita appeared suddenly in a rustic, sparsely furnished cabin. She took a step forward, stopping the strange inertia that had pulled her there, and all the water on her body fell off in droplets as if repelled by her skin. The droplets evaporated in the air, never reaching the ground. Nita stood still for a moment, trying to understand what had happened. Just when the water was about to reach her, she had felt her body being pulled forward, and then the rocky wall in front of her had disappeared, and the cabin had taken its place. She looked at her bracelet: the charm was still there, intact. Her clothes were dry, but dirty. *I'm going to get in trouble for that,* she thought, completely unaware of the commotion her disappearance had caused.

She glanced around the cabin and was surprised to see two hunting rifles lying on the mantle above the fireplace. There was a strong smell of firewood. In the middle of the room there were two small couches with a coffee table between them. She didn't see a television. The furnishings were mostly nondescript, except for a huge stuffed owl that loomed over the fireplace. It seemed to be alive. There was a tear-off calendar next to the owl, where she read the date: August sixteenth. There were lots of old-looking objects she had never seen before on the walls, beams and shelves.

She took a step toward the couches and froze in fear at the terrible sight of Anttón's lifeless body. His throat had been ripped out and his unseeing eyes were wide open. Suddenly she couldn't breathe, and her heart began to pound, as if it were trying to force her frozen body to move by pumping harder. Then someone or something moved in the shadows, snapping Nita out of her trance and making all the hairs on her body stand up. She couldn't see anything, but she could hear someone breathing. Nita turned around slowly and saw the door to the cabin. After taking one last look at the shadows, she darted toward the door. As she ran, her heart racing, she heard furniture crash behind her as someone tried to catch her. But she knew how to escape, and fast: she grasped the charm, which was glowing as if it knew her intentions, and then pushed it into the keyhole in the door as soon as she reached it. Suddenly everything went dark, and she was safe from whatever it was that was chasing her.

Nita couldn't see anything. She tripped over something and fell. After all the activity of the last few hours, her whole body was sore. She was trying to be quiet, but she couldn't help letting out a yelp of pain. A light turned on. Nita, blinking her eyes, found herself looking at a bedroom that seemed familiar. She had been there before.

"Nita!" shouted a surprised and very confused Jaime. "What are you doing here? How did you get here?" he asked in shock. He was in his underwear, as it was August and the heat made it hard to sleep at night. The only way to stay comfortable was to take the sheets off the bed and wear little or no clothing to bed.

"Jaime!" Nita couldn't believe her eyes. Her very long day caught up to her then, and she burst into tears as she threw herself into the arms of her stunned friend. "You wouldn't believe what happened to me," she sighed. "I'm so tired." Nita relaxed in his arms and fell asleep. Jaime stood there, frozen, unsure what to do.

4 THIS IS NO GAME

Adela watched her daughter from the foot of the bed. She couldn't believe that her little girl had shown up at her friend Jaime's house. She still hadn't been able to get José to give her a clear explanation of how exactly Nita had disappeared on Mount Ulía. His story was hazy, confusing, but then again so was everything that had happened in the last couple of days. She was certain of one thing: she would never leave her daughter's side again, never let her out of her sight. She was fooling herself, of course. She knew that was impossible, but she had good reason to want to keep her daughter close. The agony she had felt for the twelve hours the search lasted was the worst feeling she had ever experienced.

It was eleven o'clock in the morning now and her daughter was sleeping peacefully. She had a few bruises, but she was in perfect health. Adela sat on a chair next to the bed and studied her daughter's pretty face. Nita began to stir. "Hi, Ama," she said sleepily. Her mother looked at her lovingly.

"Hi, txiki. How are you feeling?" she asked softly, her voice showing her concern.

"I'm a little tired, and my whole body hurts," she answered. "I'm really sore all over the place. Ouch," she winced as she tried to sit up in bed. After she sat up she smiled at her mother.

"You should get some more rest," said Adela. She was concerned that Nita was feeling sore, because it meant that she had gotten a lot of exercise the day before. She must have done a lot of running last night.

"I had a nightmare," Nita said tentatively. "I was on Mount Ulía with José and a huge animal scooped me up in his mouth and brought me to Jaizkibel." The words fell like cannonballs on Adela's ears. The joy she felt at having her daughter back was replaced with deep dismay.

"What do you remember from last night?" she asked, not wanting to hear the answer. She wanted to forget the past, the pain she went through with her mother, but she knew that the past forms part of our lives, that it's always present. She braced herself for a story that would confirm that her daughter had the same strange, hopeless illness her mother suffered from in her final years, which had been the culmination of a life speckled with embarrassing and much-talked-about episodes.

"I don't remember much . . ." replied Nita. She wasn't exactly lying, but she wasn't telling the whole truth. When she saw her mother's face she realized that it hadn't been a dream. It had all been real, even if there were some things that she couldn't explain. But she didn't want to upset her mother. "Everything was dark, and I couldn't wake up," she continued, which was true: many times last night she had thought that she had to be dreaming, and she had pinched herself to see if she would wake up in the comfort of her bed. Now that she thought of it, she had fallen from a great height, she had almost drowned, she had almost gotten her throat ripped out, and she hadn't woken up: clearly, it hadn't been a dream.

"Get some rest, honey." Adela gave her a kiss and a big hug that made the little girl, whose aches from yesterday's incredible adventure were increasing by the minute, wince in pain. But she could deal with the pain, and anyway it served as tangible proof of everything she had been through. She realized that she was lucky to have escaped with only sore muscles and a few bruises. "I'll stay with you for a while if you want," said her mother, smiling. Nita smiled back. "Or are you hungry?" The memory of last night's search in the dark came back to Adela. She realized that her daughter probably hadn't eaten anything since yesterday. Nita nodded.

"Put your robe on and I'll make you some breakfast," said Adela, beginning to relax a little. She gave her daughter another kiss on the cheek and left the room.

Sitting on her bed, Nita began to go over what had happened the night before. She thought of the incredible beast she had fed. The last time she saw him, he had been asleep on the rocks. Had he survived the crashing waves? Suddenly the horrifying image of Anttón covered in blood came rushing into her head, along with the memory of that creature hiding in the shadows, watching her. She was lucky she had that key . . . wait a minute. Nita started when she realized that both her wrists were bare. Where was her bracelet, her savior, the reason she was alive to have breakfast with her mother?

She looked everywhere for the beloved treasure she had inherited from her grandmother, but she couldn't find it anywhere. She stopped to think, mentally retracing her steps. She suddenly remembered that she had ended up in Jaime's room. *I must have dropped it there,* she told herself, but her whole aching body was telling her that someone or something had taken it from her. How had she gotten to her room? And why had she appeared in Jaime's room, anyway? Why hadn't the key brought her to her own room, where she would be surrounded by her loved ones? The image of Gom looking through her window when he paid her a visit two nights before came into her head then: maybe her house wasn't the safest place in town. She had subconsciously chosen to end her adventure in the safest place she knew of, Jaime's bedroom. His room was on the sixth floor of one of the newest buildings in town. She suspected that that must be the reason she had ended up in Jaime's room. She was just beginning to discover her extraordinary gifts and the possibilities that her magic key held.

She started to search for the bracelet again, looking under the bed, in the drawers of her nightstand, in her wardrobe, until her gaze landed on the African masks on her wall. She narrowed her eyes. When she stepped away from them she sensed that she was moving away from what she was looking for, but she looked behind both masks and found nothing. Then she placed her palm against the wall behind them and her eyes widened in surprise as it dawned on her that the bracelet wasn't in her room, but there was something behind that wall, in her mother's room. Young, naive Nita didn't think to worry about this new, intense need for the strange bracelet. Two days ago she hadn't even known it existed. All she had cared about was the summer and playing outside. Now the thought of losing the bracelet was giving her a stomach ache.

Nita went out into the hallway and looked around. The coast was clear. She walked to her mother's door and checked that the room was empty before walking in. There was a chair sitting near the wall that the two rooms shared, a pile of José and Adela's clothes arranged on top of it. She didn't have to look very hard to find the bracelet in the pocket of José's jacket. She examined the bracelet, flooded with relief at having found it.

"How are you feeling?" asked José from the doorway. "I see you found the bracelet," he said calmly. "I put it away for safe keeping," he assured Nita, who had stiffened when she heard his voice. She had no reason not to trust him, but something about the situation had made her tense up.

"Your mother says you can go down for breakfast," said José, turning to go downstairs.

"José, do you know the old man we saw yesterday?" Nita asked. Her question caught him off guard.

"His name is Anttón. And you should stay away from

him," he answered, his voice tense. "Do you hear me, Nita? Don't go anywhere near him," he ordered. Nita looked at him, her face serious. She had never heard him talk like that before. "All he's done since he got to this town is get drunk and get into fights. He's dangerous," he continued, his voice softer now. "Do you understand me?" he asked in a fatherly way. Nita nodded.

The little family had a second breakfast with Nita, as her night of adventures meant she had missed the first meal of the day. They ate mostly in silence, which was broken only by Nita thanking her mother for the breakfast that she gobbled up greedily. There was a tense moment after breakfast when Nita asked her mother if she could go outside, but Adela still couldn't let her little girl out of her sight after what they had been through the day before. She firmly told her she would be staying inside for the rest of the day. She could watch TV or play with her toys. But suddenly Nita found all the objects that had given her so many hours of entertainment and fun totally useless. Nothing could compete with her magic key, her grandmother's bracelet, and she was dying to tell her friends about it. She didn't mention this to her mother and José. They wouldn't believe her anyway, and she didn't want her mother to get mad at her like she had the day before.

Nita sat down and began to draw the cabin where Anttón had been murdered and the strange beast in the shadows. But she didn't have a clear picture of the creature because she hadn't gotten a good look at it: she had been more interested in getting out of there than in finding out what Anttón's killer looked like. Suddenly her ears perked up as she heard her mother and José talking. Adela had gone out to buy bread earlier that morning and Anttón had approached her to ask after Nita. José was clearly upset to hear about the encounter, and he began to rant about Anttón. The old man was dangerous, he said, and he told Adela he thought they should all stay away from him. Nita heard them say that the police had called off their search when she turned up at her friend's house. Nita was surprised by what she heard. Anttón was alive, but that didn't make any sense, given her memories from the night before. And she hadn't realized that Adela and José had reported her disappearance to the police.

Nita replayed her memories from the cabin over and over again in her head and drew everything she could remember. The cabin felt strangely familiar to her, but it was different now, maybe messier, she thought. She had been there before. She drew the big owl on the mantle, along with a few of the objects she had seen, the couches, and even the calendar that was hanging next to the stuffed bird. As she drew the number sixteen, she had a sudden revelation. She ran into the kitchen to check the date. The family had a large monthly wall calendar given out by a local bank every year, showing colorful scenes of Basque villages and farmers. The calendar was open to the month of August, and she found the sixteenth, but she couldn't remember what day of the week it was.

"Ama, what's the date?" she asked, staring at the calendar.

"August fifteenth. Why?" answered Adela, slightly puzzled by her daughter's question.

Nita ran up to her room without a word.

Adela went to the coffee table in the living room where Nita had been drawing and was shocked by what she saw. The drawing wasn't perfect, but Adela instantly recognized the place. There was the fireplace, and the owl. She had spent so many nights full of joy and pleasure in front of that fireplace, sharing caresses, kisses and orgasms, making plans and whispering her deepest secrets to Raúl, Nita's father. Suddenly an intense burning pain in her stomach brought back the anguish she had lived through just before her mother's dementia started. This particular pain was so familiar to her that she didn't even wince when she felt it again. Many theories had been thrown around regarding Raúl's disappearance: one was that he had gotten tired of family life, another was that he was involved in some plot related to ETA, an armed terrorist group that wanted Basque independence from Spain, and there were other hypotheses. But none of them made sense to those who knew Raúl, who was wholly committed to his little family.

In all those hours they had spent at his cabin, Adela and Raúl had talked politics, the environment, everything, and Adela knew he was completely against using violence to achieve independence. In fact, Adela was the more revolutionary of the two, and she was far from radical. At the time it was quite common for supporters of Basque independence to flee to other countries, especially if they had been accused, wrongly or rightly, of having ties to ETA. They would disappear overnight, but they always sent word of where they were, which, though good for their families, often had devastating consequences for them. Various groups associated with the independence movement in some way had approached her to ask where Raúl was. Nobody knew.

She remembered his smile, his eyes, which would light up when they saw her, the scent of his shaving cream, the smell of his shirts, his kisses. Even on his worst day he was the light of her life. But then he left, and he took her happiness with him. Just like that, he destroyed everything they had built. Even through her agony, Adela had seen that Nita needed a father figure, and just as Raúl disappeared, two years later José appeared in her life. He was a wonderful man and he even reminded her of Raúl, but he could never fill the void left by her lost love.

Upstairs in her room, Nita was thinking about what had happened in the cabin the night before. Could the calendar in the cabin have been wrong, or had she really seen the future, the terrible future that awaited Anttón? What should she do? Talk to her mother? José? The police? She felt sick with worry. What was she thinking? Was she going crazy? Why did she feel the need to help the town drunk? And what was that monster in the shadows? And where had Gom come from? Her mother hadn't believed anything she had told her about what had happened in the last two days, and she also felt the need to protect her from whatever was going on. With a deep sigh, she thought of her grandmother. Though her memory of her had already faded, she was sure her grandmother would know what to do, how to help her. The bracelet had been hers, after all.

She told herself to calm down and began to draw conclusions about what had happened. She had been thinking of Jaime's room when she put the charm in the keyhole at the cabin, and then she appeared there. The first time she had used the key, on the cliff, her mind was blank: all she was thinking about was holding on to the rock. She had appeared in the cabin, a place that she had been to before, although she had forgotten it. A few days ago her only worry was whether she could go outside to play with her friends, go to the beach or go hiking, and the only drama in her life came when the weather was bad and she couldn't do the things she loved. This was all crazy. No one would believe her. No one except . . . her friends. They were the only ones she could confide in.

Nita told her mother that she needed to rest. They agreed that she should lie down until lunchtime. Back in her room, she arranged some pillows under the sheets, went to her bedroom door with the bracelet in her hand, and realized that the door didn't have a keyhole. She went to the window: no keyhole there either. She had just decided to sneak out of the house the old-fashioned way when she had an idea. She went to her wardrobe and sure enough, there was a keyhole in the door. The wardrobe had never been locked, as far as she knew, but the bracelet reacted: the charm took on the shape of the keyhole. Nita put the key into the lock and disappeared from the room.

Jaime and Amaya were on the promenade near the harbor, talking about what had happened to Nita. Jaime told Amaya how startled he had been to find her in his room.

"I bet she went there because she likes you," teased Amaya.

"No she doesn't!" Jaime shot back. He blushed: it would be nice if that were true. He thought of the look of confusion on his father's face when he had seen Nita in his son's room, which had quickly turned into a proud smile that he tried and failed to hide when he decided that Jaime and Nita must be dating. Any other explanation was unthinkable; he would never have believed what really happened. "Nobody saw her come in. She just appeared there," continued a perplexed Jaime.

"People don't just appear magically," argued Amaya. "What, did she get that huge monster that almost ate you to take her there?" she suggested with sarcasm. Jaime hadn't thought of that. Maybe the beast had thrown her in through the window or something. *Those teeth,* he thought, as a shiver ran down his back at the memory of the beast. *And the size of that thing! Why hadn't Amaya seen it? Had he just imagined it?* They were the same questions that had been bugging him for the last couple of days.

"Hi, guys," said Nita, startling her friends.

"Hi, Nita!" said Amaya enthusiastically, giving a little jump of excitement. She hugged her friend.

"Hi, Nita. Are you feeling better?" said Jaime. He felt a little uncomfortable. He didn't know if he should give her a hug or just wave. Nita solved the problem for him when she threw her arms around him.

"I have so much to tell you guys," she said, her voice low. She was worried. If her friends didn't believe her when she told them about all the crazy things she went through yesterday, she would be completely alone.

She began by telling them how angry her mother had been with her when she got home after their unsuccessful hunting trip, and then she described her adventure on Ulía and how she had ended up on Mount Jaizkibel. She paused to catch her breath and continued her incredible story. Her friends listened in awe as she described everything that had happened in such detail that they could feel the waves crashing on the rocks—they were in the harbor, after all—and feel the presence of the monster in the shadows. It was all so exciting, like watching a Hollywood movie unfold before them. Amaya was the first to say something.

"I think I saw the old man today, but he wasn't drunk this time," she said, contradicting Nita's story of Anttón's murder.

"I know, my mom talked to him this morning," answered Nita. She didn't mind that Amaya had some questions about her story. She had always thought of Amaya as the smartest of the group, and she was the first to admit that lots of yesterday's events didn't make sense. "I think . . ." Nita paused, trying to find a way to explain her interpretation of what she had seen. "Really, I guess I have a *feeling* that something bad is going to happen to the old man, to Anttón."

"You saw him dead at the cabin," said Jaime.

"But he's alive," Amaya reminded him.

"I don't know what's going to happen, or when, but I have a feeling it's going to be soon," Nita insisted. "I need your help," she said, urgency in her voice.

The three friends agreed that they couldn't tell anyone about what had happened. It sounded too crazy. But Nita was very important to Jaime and Amaya, and they decided to help her on her mission. But before she would help, Amaya needed to see some proof that backed up her friend's story. Jaime didn't need to see anything; he had seen too much already and he was sure that Nita was telling the truth.

Nita checked to make sure that no one was around and began to wave her arm. She had to draw five circles before a smoke ring appeared in front of the children. Jaime stared at it in awe, but Amaya didn't see anything. She put her hand out in front of her, but she couldn't feel anything either. Then she waved her hand in frustration, inadvertently brushing the ring away. She felt a sharp pain, like a static shock, and pulled her hand back. Even after a few seconds, it still stung. Amaya couldn't wrap her head around what had just happened, but *something* had happened, so she decided to play along with her friends.

The plan was simple: they would follow Anttón for as long as they could. Jaime added a touch of sophistication to their mission by running home to get his walkie-talkies, a Christmas gift from two years before. They split up into two teams: Amaya and Nita would work together and Jaime would go solo. Each group would take a walkie-talkie. They agreed that they would be able to keep tabs on Anttón by setting up just two stakeout points: Pasai San Pedro was a small town, after all. One team would set up camp by the promenade that ran along the harbor, near the entrance to the main path leading up Ulía. The other would keep a lookout in the center of town.

Amaya had seen Anttón that morning, so she knew where to find him: sure enough, he was sitting quietly on a bench in a park, watching people walk by. He was leaning on a walking stick. The children had never seen him with a walking stick before, but if he had really been going up and down Mount Ulía it made sense that he would need some extra support. But as determined as they were to watch the old man's every move, they were children, and they had to be home for lunch at two, so their surveillance work had to be put on hold at lunchtime.

Nita said goodbye to her friends. Then she found a garage in a quiet area and put the charm into the lock on the door. She appeared suddenly in her bedroom. She took the pillows out from under the sheets and went out into the hallway. She had a quiet lunch with her mother and José. When they finished eating, she asked her mother if she could go for a walk with her friends, but Adela told her to stay inside and rest for the rest of the day. The summer was far from over and she'd have plenty of time to play the next day. Nita had a plan, so she didn't put up much of a fight. Genuinely tired from the morning's detective work, she yawned, which gave her a great excuse for staying in her room that afternoon. She told her mother and José she wanted to take a nap until dinner. She stretched and let out a little whimper of pain in front of them. Her little body was still very sore from the night before.

After lunch Nita went upstairs for her nap. She set up the pillows again and used her key to sneak out through the wardrobe. The afternoon heat was oppressive, but the three friends were ready to take up where they had left off. They switched positions: Jaime would watch the promenade and the girls would go to the center of town. It didn't take long for Anttón to sit down on the same bench he had occupied that morning. It almost looked like he was waiting for something. The girls used their walkie-talkie to report back to Jaime, whose own report consisted of a description of the ice cream cone he was eating. Then Anttón stood up, and Amaya and Nita began to follow him. They were forced to regroup when they discovered that Anttón had his own mission: to follow Nita's mother. Nita gave a start when she saw Adela looking through the window of one of the many stores in town that closed in the afternoons in August. The store was right across from the bench the old man had been sitting on. After glancing through the window Adela headed toward a popular bar in town to have a cup of coffee and read the paper. Apparently, the old man they were watching was watching Nita's mother. A little alarm went off in Nita's head: this seemed more like a ritual than a coincidence. The girls had planned to follow Anttón together, but Nita asked Amaya to go on alone. She couldn't risk her mother seeing her.

She stood at the opening of a dead-end alley that local children had nicknamed *"la tapia"* and watched from afar as her friend observed Adela and Anttón from behind the corner of a building on the next block. Amaya watched Nita's mother sit down at one of the tables set up outside the bar, a newspaper in her hand. Anttón walked by the bar and stopped to say hello to Adela.

Jaime was in the harbor finishing up his chocolate ice cream cone, a welcome treat in the hot August sun, when two shadows suddenly darkened his view of the water. They belonged to Jon and Lander, the two bullies who had sparked the formation of Nita's tight-knit group of friends. Jon was the leader of the two, due to the fact that he had a slightly higher degree of initiative than Lander; unfortunately he used it mostly to find ways to pick on his classmates.

Jon was thin, a little taller than average, and full of nervous energy. His aggressive behavior was a result of his lack of emotional intelligence. The small dark-haired girl in his class, Nita, made him very nervous. He actually liked her, but he didn't know how to deal with his feelings, so he tried to show off with absurd demonstrations of his brute strength. He loved to brag about his older brother, who was known for participating in the pro-independence demonstrations in the region. But Jon knew enough not to brag to his brother about his own "accomplishments" because he knew he wouldn't like that he picked on people.

He and Lander had found Jaime, but Jon had actually gone to the promenade looking for Nita. He had seen her there with Jaime and Amaya that morning, and he wanted to talk to her, although he didn't know what he would say. To his surprise and frustration, all he found there was the stupid fat kid. Nita was nowhere in sight. But he had something to settle with the fat kid anyway.

"Hey, sack of lard," he smirked. Jaime looked at him nervously. In a fistfight the little bully wouldn't stand a chance against Jaime, but Jon had honed his aggressive pose. He knew it was very intimidating to the other kids.

A gust of wind blew into the alleyway where Nita was hiding, and pieces of paper, plastic and cardboard began to fly around. Nita noticed the change in the air and turned her attention toward the inside of the alleyway, her surveillance mission momentarily forgotten. Gom appeared in the sky above her. The enormous creature descended and came to a stop a few feet above the ground, where he hovered. The beast was even more impressive than usual, glowing with healthy energy.

"Hello, little one," he said, his voice serious. Nita regarded him carefully. Gom could see that she was still frightened of him. "Don't be scared. I'm on your side. You saved my life," he said firmly.

"Why are you here?" asked Nita cautiously.

"I came to warn you. I smelled him," he answered, and she could hear worry in his voice. "He's close," he said, looking all around.

"Who's close?" asked Nita, intrigued.

"The son of shadows and mud, the Nobusk of the East," he said, lowering his eyes at the memory of past battles.

"Is he like you?" asked Nita fearfully.

"No!" Gom answered immediately. He was offended. "He's a terrible, frightening beast, and he is Her servant, like so many others," he said. Nita tried to contain her surprise at Gom's choice of words: she would have used the same ones to describe him.

"Whose servant?" she asked, even more intrigued.

Gom looked around again before bringing his face in close to Nita's. "Her name is the Root," he whispered, but his normal tone of voice was so loud that the whisper could be heard from quite far away anyway. "She's older than the mountains, and the oceans," he continued in the same hushed tone. "And she knows you exist. I don't know how she found out, but she knows."

Nita furrowed her brow. "So what can I do?" she asked. He was scaring her.

"You can't run from his shadow or escape from the mud he'll create around you. There's no other way: you have to fight," said Gom sadly.

"Will you help me?" asked the little girl.

"I will spend the rest of my days here by your side. I couldn't survive without you. Of course I'll help you, my little one. I'll do whatever you ask. Every fiber of my being, down to the last scale and pore on my skin, will obey your wishes," declared the huge animal, puffing with pride.

Nita didn't understand exactly what they were up against, but she felt better knowing that the giant beast was on her side.

"Hi. Guess who has your fat little friend?" crackled Jon's mocking voice over the walkie-talkie. Nita stared at the device in her hand. "Give it back!" she heard Jaime say in the background.

"Jon, what's the matter with you? Why are you being so stupid?" she asked angrily.

"Uhh . . . How about if I make your little friend eat his walkie-talkie?" Jon tried to take back control of the conversation. "There's lots of room in that fat belly."

"What exactly do you want?" asked Nita, exasperated.

"I didn't like how things ended the last time I saw you and I want to hear you apologize," ordered the bully. That wasn't the real reason he wanted to see her, but communication wasn't his strong suit.

Nita looked at the beast in front of her and she had an idea. A wicked grin spread across her face.

"Do your balls still hurt?" she teased loudly.

"I'm gonna to kick your—I'm gonna—" Jon sputtered, losing control.

"I'm in *la tapia*, you coward!" shouted Nita. "Come get your balls back!" she finished with a cocky laugh.

Jon's face screwed up in rage and he threw the walkie-talkie on the ground, where the plastic casing broke into pieces. Jaime clicked his tongue in disappointment. He ran to pick up his walkie-talkie while Jon and his crony ran off to the alleyway to prove how manly they were by beating up a little girl.

Nita called to Amaya from the opening of the alleyway, bringing her friend out of the state of deep concentration she had been in for the last few minutes. Amaya didn't know what Nita was up to, but she headed toward the alleyway. She didn't see how just at that moment, something tried to grab Anttón's arm and the old man, surprised and frightened, ran off as best as he could.

She didn't see anyone when she got to the alleyway. The five-ton gomulus was right in front of her, but she couldn't see him. He flew away when she arrived. Amaya ventured into the alleyway, but all she saw were a lot of dumpsters and the back doors of the businesses in the surrounding buildings. She turned around and was nearly scared to death by Nita, who had appeared suddenly. She was holding something strange in her hands.

Jaime was scowling at what was left of his walkie-talkie. He couldn't get it to work. With a sigh, he began to gather all the broken pieces. Just when he was turning to go find Nita, he saw Anttón running into the parking garage that had just been constructed under a new apartment building. There was a strange figure following close behind him, sliding in the bushes and shadows in front of the building. Whatever it was followed Anttón into the garage. Jaime looked on, intrigued. It was risky, but he could watch from a distance and tell Nita what he saw. Maybe they would finally get some answers in this darn game. Until now all he had to show for playing was a broken walkie-talkie.

Jon and Lander, panting, arrived at the alleyway expecting to find Nita, but there didn't seem to be anyone there. Jon looked over his shoulder, but there was no one behind them. He had assumed Nita might try to sneak up on them, but everything was quiet. The boys moved farther into the alleyway and stopped in front of one of the dumpsters. They heard a low growling sound and tensed nervously.

"Come on, Nita, get out of there or you'll be sorry!" said Jon firmly.

Suddenly Nita, her face covered by one of her African masks, shot out of the dumpster and fired a cloud of smoke that she had made in her hiding spot at the boys, who felt an electric shock that made them let out high-pitched squeals. They sounded like little girls. As a finishing touch, Nita improvised a fierce lion's roar. They stumbled back in fear and were greeted on the other side by Amaya, who was wearing the other mask. Both boys lost their balance, then scrambled to their feet and ran off.

The girls burst out laughing. The plan had worked, thanks to Nita's bracelet and her magic key. Nita took off the mask that used to hang on her wall as she shook with laughter. Suddenly an ambulance tore by on the main road that ran through town, sirens wailing. It was headed in the direction of Jaime's stakeout spot. Nita had a feeling. A bad feeling. She stopped laughing suddenly, threw her mask on the ground and ran after the ambulance, leaving a confused Amaya standing there alone. The girl picked up her friend's mask and watched her run off.

By the time Nita reached the ambulance it was parked, and a crowd of people had gathered around it. She gasped as she saw that the paramedics were loading Jaime into the ambulance on a stretcher. She couldn't believe this was happening. She ran up to the ambulance, but the paramedics wouldn't let her get close to Jaime. He was unconscious, but he didn't appear to have a single scratch on his body. Nita couldn't hold back tears of pain when she saw her friend. Something beyond the crowd of people caught her eye then: it was Anttón, and he was hurrying away, eyes darting nervously. The walkie-talkie Nita was wearing on her belt screeched briefly and some people in the crowd looked in her direction. Tears streaming down her face, she stumbled away from the very spot where she and her friends had started to play what they thought was a harmless game. It had turned into something more.

5 THE REALITY OF REVENGE

Alone in her dark room, Nita was curled up on her bed, crying over her friend. She had teleported to her room using the magic key, but her mind had been whirling from the shock of seeing Jaime hurt. It had taken her longer to arrive than ever before, which confirmed her suspicion that her mental state influenced where she ended up.

Who could do this to Jaime? He's the nicest person in the world, she thought, trying to push aside what had to be the worst feeling she had ever felt: guilt. *It's all my fault. If I hadn't gotten him involved in this . . .* She couldn't stop torturing herself, replaying everything that had happened since Gom came to see her. She realized then that she had put her two best friends in danger multiple times in the last two days. *And why? Because I was curious,* she thought, an unbearable ache squeezing her stomach and spreading to her heart. She heard a noise downstairs and tiptoed to the stairwell to see what was going on. She could hear Adela and José talking.

"People in town are saying that Jaime got into an accident, that he's in a coma," Adela said to José, her voice low.

"What? What happened?" he asked, worried.

"Nobody really knows. Someone found him on the floor of the garage in the new apartment building. He had a toy with him. One of those radios, you know, a walkie-talkie, and it was broken. But he didn't have any broken bones, and there was no blood or anything," explained Adela.

"They didn't find anyone else there with him?" he asked with interest.

"I don't know," replied Adela, shaking her head. She had given him all the information she had, and it wasn't much.

From her perch on the stairs, Nita heard José's question loud and clear, and she thought of Jaime lying on the stretcher while Anttón fled the scene. Yes, someone else had been there with Jaime. The old drunk they were trying to help was clearly to blame for Jaime getting hurt.

"Are you going to tell Nita?" José asked, sounding worried.

"Is she still asleep?" asked Adela.

"Yeah. She hasn't come down at all," replied José.

Adela thought for a moment. "No, I'll tell her tomorrow when she wakes up. She's been through so much already these last couple of days."

Nita went back up to her room and waited until Adela and José went to bed. Her mind was whirring with ways she could make the old drunk pay for what he had done to Jaime. Her heart was beating so fast she thought it might burst through her chest. Rage coursed through her little body, and it was suddenly inevitable: an eleven-year-old girl in possession of an enormous magical beast was a ticking time bomb subject to the whims and naiveté characteristic of all children her age. Nita jumped out of bed and thrust her key into the wardrobe.

She appeared by the harbor and started to run along the promenade, waving her right hand, where she wore her bracelet. She left a trail of thick smoke in her wake, which she knew would attract the enormous beast. Soon she felt the fantastic animal at her back, gobbling up her smoke signals. He came to a stop in front of her and without hesitating, Nita jumped onto his back and used the chains there to pull herself up onto his right shoulder. She held on tightly to one of the chains on his face. The animal took flight, the girl on his shoulder.

A terrified Anttón was tearing through the woods, clutching his walking stick. He knew there was no way out and no place to hide. He was too old to run like this; he felt like his body could explode any minute now. Even if he somehow managed to survive what was coming, it would take him weeks to recover from the exertion. He had to keep moving, to keep going until dawn, if he wanted to have the slightest chance at survival. A deep growl made him jump in fear but he didn't stop running. He was used to being in danger. He had been in danger his whole life.

The enormous beast and the little girl were flying over the dark waters where the Pasajes River met the sea. They took a sharp turn and headed up Mount Ulía to look for the old man. Nita scanned the ground in search of the vermin that had put her friend in a coma. A mixture of guilt and impotence were tearing her up, pushing the devastated girl toward a horrible act that would undoubtedly leave her traumatized, scarred for the rest of her life. No one suspected Anttón's involvement in what had happened to Jaime, and no one cared about the old man's fate. The pain and anger rushing through her body were telling her to take action, to punish him for what he had done, but the eleven-year-old, who had never witnessed true suffering, whose experience of the world was limited to a tiny sphere in which her main concerns revolved around what game she and her friends would play, couldn't possibly understand the ramifications of what she was planning to do. She might wish for his death, or for Gom to hurt him, without grasping the radical difference between the two punishments. She was still just a child.

Using Gom's sense of smell as a guide, they finally spotted Anttón deep within the forest. He was running desperately through the woods, ducking under hanging branches and darting to avoid trees and plants that stood between him and salvation.

Anttón emerged from the dense forest into a circular clearing. When he reached the middle of the clearing he paused for a moment, panting and looking up at the starry night sky. Gom's silhouette cutting across the sky caught his eye and he spun around, trying to follow the dark figure with his gaze, but he lost sight of him. When he turned around the huge beast was landing right in front of him.

"Thank God!" Anttón exclaimed with a smile of relief, which quickly disappeared when he saw Nita on Gom's right shoulder.

Anttón studied them, his face grim. Then, seeming to remember that he was running from something, he looked over his shoulder. Then he grasped the end of his walking stick and pulled, making the stick longer. The newly exposed portion of the stick glowed with a bright light that illuminated most of the clearing. The old man took two steps forward and plunged the walking stick into the ground.

"Stop him!" Nita ordered her giant sidekick.

Gom grabbed the old man and lifted him up until he was face to face with Nita.

"Why did you hurt him?" sobbed Nita. This was the moment to take her revenge, but she had gotten a strange feeling when she saw the old man, and something inside her was making her waver.

"No, it wasn't me!" Anttón assured her.

"There was no one else there! We were following you!" Nita said through her tears. "I saw you die. We were trying to help you!" screamed Nita, her face twisted in rage.

Anttón regarded her in surprise, but then turned away suddenly and shouted to Gom, "Do you smell him?"

The huge beast looked around, very agitated.

"Little one, he's here!" he said to his new friend.

"What are you talking about? The old man has to pay for what he did!" Nita, focused on revenge, was barely aware of what was going on.

Gom set Anttón back on the ground and Nita, confused and angry, launched herself off of Gom toward the old man. "He has to pay!" she sobbed as she flew through the air at him.

Nita crashed into Anttón, and they both fell to the ground. Now on top of him, she alternately banged her fists against him desperately and dropped her head against his tired chest, sobbing.

"That boy saved my life," croaked Anttón sadly. The little girl wasn't strong enough to hurt an adult the size of Anttón, so the only pain he felt came from seeing her so desperately sad and angry with him. Little by little the blows began to lose strength. Nita finally rested her head on Anttón's chest and shot an accusing look at Gom.

"You're supposed to obey me," she said angrily.

"He's my friend," replied the beast, bowing his head.

A loud howl interrupted the argument. Both Gom and Anttón looked around apprehensively. Anttón leapt to his feet with a grace that surprised Nita and then helped her up.

"It's the Nobusk of the East," Gom said nervously. "That was his victory cry. He knows he's going to defeat us. We're in his element, the darkness," he continued as he paced in uneasy circles around Nita and Anttón.

"It's too late," Anttón choked out as he looked at the walking stick he had planted in the ground.

"We'll fight!" shouted Gom firmly. The mood lifted slightly: with a beast of his size on their side, they might have a chance.

No sooner were the words out of his mouth than a shadow just beyond the circle of light cast by the old man's walking stick dragged him off into the darkness. Gom scratched at the ground, leaving claw marks in the dirt. Anttón and Nita could hear the sounds of two enormous beasts fighting: grunts, blows, and branches and trees snapping. They stood in the clearing, turning their heads to follow the sounds of the fight. Anttón grabbed Nita and croaked, "Stay in the light." Nita looked at him, her eyes wide with fear, face streaked with dirt and tears. She nodded in silence. It was dawning on her that she had had it all wrong, that she shouldn't have tried to hurt Anttón. The old man wasn't running from them, but from something darker than the night, something that was following him, trying to kill him.

Suddenly a barely conscious Gom was tumbling through the air above the circle of light. Anttón dived to one side and Nita to the other to avoid being hit by the giant beast barreling toward them at full speed. Gom crashed to the ground, uprooting the old man's walking stick and dragging it with him. When the beast finally skidded to a halt beyond the clearing, the dense vegetation swallowed the light and it was even darker than before.

"Get out of here! I've got him right where I want him," Gom mumbled from where he lay, about to lose consciousness.

In that moment, Nita, who had already scrambled to her feet, finally got a glimpse of the Nobusk of the East. The creature's underside was similar to that of a slug, but it seemed to be made up of mud and black sand. The top half of the dark beast was a mess of tentacles that ended in mouths, which he used to grab and crush anything he could. At first Nita counted six tentacles, but then she thought there were at least ten. They appeared and disappeared in the mass of his body.

The beast moved past Nita, who held her breath while she watched him glide toward Gom, his main opponent, for the time being at least. He nearly slid over the small patch of light formed by the walking stick, but at the last minute he pulled back from it as if in pain. When he was about to reach Gom, Anttón called out to him. "I'm over here, you bastard!" He was trying to put an end to the fight. If he sacrificed himself he could save the girl and Gom, who had fought so faithfully by his side for many years. Gom would teach Nita everything she needed to know about her destiny. The beast turned away from Gom and went for the old man, grabbing him with three of his mouths.

Anttón braced himself for the terrible pain of being ripped

apart in the many jaws of the beast, but the nobusk suddenly let out a howl and shook with pain. Nita had thrown the glowing walking stick at him from behind, and the light had burned the skin-like covering on his back. He spun around swiftly, forgetting Anttón, and turned on the girl, carefully avoiding the illuminated walking stick. The son of shadows and mud brought his many mouths close to Nita as if to study her. When he got close to the bracelet on the girl's right wrist he jumped back in fear. But it took the beast only a few seconds to recover and lunge at Nita. She was saved by Gom, who had recovered from the first round of the fight. He jumped on his enemy and for a moment the two beasts disappeared into a twisted mass, before the nobusk sent Gom flying through the air again. The farther away they moved from the light, the more unstoppable the nobusk became.

Anttón ran toward Nita, but he didn't make it. The creature swatted at him with one of his long tentacles and he fell to the ground. Nita would have to face the beast alone. The nobusk approached her again, more wary this time, but he came closer than he had before. Nita saw something moving inside the monster then. It looked like a hand, a child's hand, and it was clawing, trying to get out of there. Suddenly she saw the outline of a face against the upper part of the beast's body. "Jaime!" she screamed in surprise. And then one of the nobusk's tentacles pierced Nita's stomach, and she was frozen.

Adela jolted awake, a cold sweat covering her body. Once again the feeling that something was terribly wrong making the hairs on the back of her neck stand up. José was sleeping peacefully beside her. She watched him lying there and thought back to the last time they had made love. It seemed so long ago. The stress of the past few days had brought back the painful memory of the final years of her mother's life, so she hadn't been in the mood. She would have to fix that, but not tonight. She got out of bed to go down to the kitchen and have a glass of water, but she paused outside Nita's room. She couldn't stop thinking about what had happened to Jaime, and she wanted to tell her daughter as soon as possible, but she dreaded seeing her suffer, as she knew she would. She opened the door and looked outside. In the darkness she could just make out the shape of her daughter lying in bed. She turned back toward the stairs, lost in thought.

A blue light was shining from the spot where the nobusk's tentacle was piercing Nita. A cold pain coursed through the girl's body. She turned her eyes to the creature in front of her and again she saw Jaime's head. He was struggling to get out. "You hurt him!" she screamed at the nobusk as she used her right hand to grab the tentacle that was holding her in place. The charm on her bracelet began to glow and the beast howled in pain. Nita pulled the tentacle out of her stomach and squeezed it. The nobusk continued to howl as the tentacle she was holding began to freeze like an icicle. The enormous creature was unable to move; it was as if he were tethered to Nita. The ice was spreading toward the trunk of his body.

"No!" shouted Anttón. He hit the frozen tentacle with his walking stick, allowing the creature to pull himself free. The nobusk slid off, whimpering in pain. Nita was left holding part of the frozen tentacle. For a moment it looked like a shining sword. She didn't understand what had just happened, but the old man had clearly freed the beast that had been at her mercy only a moment before.

"Why did you do that? I had him under control!" Nita shouted angrily. Anttón looked at her in awe. He had seen a great deal in his life, but this little girl had just done something he would have never thought possible: she had nearly destroyed one of the most terrifying and dangerous beasts on the planet.

"We can't kill him," he croaked.

"He's right," said Gom, approaching the two humans. "I felt it too. We have to rescue your friend first."

Nita, wide-eyed, looked from Gom to Anttón. "Was that really Jaime inside him?" she asked.

"His life," Anttón replied with difficulty before gesturing to Gom to take over.

"Ah, yes. All right," said Gom when he realized that Anttón was asking for his help. "That dark and terrible creature has the power to keep whatever part of his prey he wants. He took Jaime's life and left his body, which is only a shell. Life is . . . it's pure energy, something we all have inside us," he explained.

To Nita it sounded like he was describing something she had learned about at church. "Is it the same as a soul?" she asked, calmer now. She was intrigued.

Gom shook his enormous head and said, "I guess you could call it that."

Nita had been caught up in one dangerous and mysterious situation after another over the past two days and she was getting tired of not knowing what was going on. "Why does that monster want to hurt me? And what does he want from Jaime?" she asked Gom, whom she might have called a monster just a day before. When he didn't answer she turned to Anttón, tears in her eyes.

"It's me he's after," croaked the exhausted old man.

Gom let out a growl. "That's impossible. I thought we had put enough distance between us," he said. "All those years of fighting, the pain we went through, staying so far away, all for nothing. Thousands of failed attempts . . . they must think we're pathetic," he lamented to the old man.

"Who thinks you're pathetic?" Nita asked, confused.

"That wicked servant of the Root and his friends. Once they feared us. But now they're laughing in your fa—"

"Shh!" Anttón interrupted. Gom fell silent.

"What did you do to the nobusk to make him want to kill you?" Nita asked the old man.

Anttón's face darkened and he gestured that it was time to go.

"Wait!" shouted Nita. "Do you know how to save Jaime?" she asked, desperate to rescue her friend.

"I'll help you," he answered, his gruff voice softening. The boy had saved his life, after all.

"Who is the Root?" Nita asked.

"The Root is the foulest of creatures, and the oldest and most powerful. May your life never be darkened by her shadow," said Gom. Something in his voice told Nita that the conversation was over.

For now, there was nothing to do but wait. They didn't know where the Nobusk of the East would go to hide. At the pace he moved he was probably miles away by now. And while he was more vulnerable during the daylight hours, like other creatures of his species the Nobusk of the East had the ability to shrink to a tenth of his normal size, allowing him to hide in the shadows. He took on his full size only at night, under the cover of darkness. Their one advantage was Gom and his excellent sense of smell.

It was almost dawn. Nita's vision of the future hadn't come true. Everything had changed the moment Jaime stood between the nobusk and the old man. Nita's heart ached at the thought of her dear friend.

Adela was finishing her glass of water and thinking about the events of the last few days and her strange attraction toward that old man, Anttón. There was something so familiar about him; the way he moved reminded her of Raúl, José, even her father. It was very unlikely that he was related to Raúl: Adela knew Raúl didn't have any living relatives. She had found that out when she set out to find the one man she had ever loved unconditionally, determined to find answers, however harsh they were, and, if necessary, to beg him on her hands and knees to come back to her. But she had found nothing. Her mother's mental illness and the overwhelming responsibility of having to raise her daughter on her own had turned her world into a cage, and there was no way out, no air to breathe. Thank God for her job with the San Sebastián City Council and for the local daycare, which had kept her afloat during that terrible time. But on occasions it was too much for her, and she would feel so hopeless, helpless, completely lost. And then she met José, who was always there for her no matter what, and she fell in love and got back much of the happiness that she had lost. Afraid to hurt him, she hadn't told José about what was bothering her now. She couldn't make sense of anything anyway, no matter how hard she thought about it.

A noise in Nita's room interrupted her thoughts. Concerned, she went upstairs to check on her daughter. The door was ajar. She was about to go into the room when she saw Nita creep up to the bed and start to remove the pillows she had set up earlier. When she moved the sheets to get at the pillows, Jaime's walkie-talkie fell to the floor. She had hidden it under the covers. She looked at it sadly, picked it up and hid it under her pillow.

Adela froze at the realization that her daughter had deceived her. But it was absurd, impossible: Adela had been in the kitchen and she hadn't seen her come in. *What is happening to my baby?* she thought, completely bewildered. She didn't know how to confront her because she didn't understand what was going on. The pillows arranged on her bed were evidence of some sort of deception, but she couldn't have left the room. It was impossible to get into the room through the window. Adela resolved to watch her daughter closely and try to help her solve whatever problem it was that she was having.

6 DON'T LEAVE ME

It was Saturday morning, and Adela and José were eating breakfast in the kitchen in silence. Soon they would have to tell Nita the bad news about Jaime. They were dreading it, because they would have to see their little girl suffer. Adding to her worries, Adela knew that something was wrong, that Nita was hiding something from her. She cleared her breakfast things and put her empty coffee cup in the sink.

"I'm going to go buy bread and the paper," said José.

"OK. We need some fruit too," replied Adela. Neither of them were feeling very talkative. Adela steeled herself and headed up to Nita's room as José left the house. He would be sure to buy some groceries later, but right now he had an entirely different plan in mind.

Nita woke up with the feeling that she still needed hours of sleep to recover from the events of the last few days and nights. Her little body had taken quite a beating, and she was sore all over. Adela walked into the room quietly and sat on the edge of the bed.

"Hi, *txiki*," she said softly.

"Mmmm . . . What is it, Ama?" asked Nita sleepily.

"Yesterday . . . your friend Jaime was in an accident." Adela forced the words out. Nita sat up suddenly, immediately alert.

"What happened to him?" she asked, hoping her mother could give her some information.

"We don't know, but he's in the hospital now, under observation." Adela left out some details to soften the news.

Nita suddenly burst into tears and threw her arms around her mother's neck. "It's all my fault," sobbed the little girl. Weeping in her mother's arms took off some of the weight of the guilt that was tormenting her. Adela was surprised by her daughter's reaction to the news.

"It wasn't anyone's fault. He was alone. He probably tripped and hit his head on something," she said, trying to calm her down.

"No, I should have been there with him!" Nita sobbed uncontrollably.

Nita cried for a few minutes before calming down enough to talk. Everything that had happened to her, everything she had discovered in the last three days, was starting to be too much. Some of her questions had been answered, but she knew her grandmother would have been able to help her understand. Adela was her daughter: maybe she knew something about all this.

"Ama, did your mother ever talk about people's spirits?" she asked, her eyes shining with tears. Her grandmother was older than her mother so perhaps she had passed down some sort of ancient wisdom. And the bracelet had belonged to her.

Adela, surprised by the question, studied her daughter's face as all the times she had been embarrassed by her mother's eccentricities came flooding back to her at once. Her stomach churned at the memories. "Your grandmother was very special," she said sadly. "But her head was very— cloudy—her whole life."

"What do you mean by cloudy?" asked Nita, confused.

"She believed in home remedies and the power of herbs. She was so good to her friends and family. Yes, she did believe that everyone has a spirit . . . well, she called it a 'life.' She used to talk about how every person, every living creature, has one," she continued as Nita listened intently. Adela wasn't going to tell her daughter about the countless times people had called her mother a witch, or the strange looks from their neighbors, or the absurd arguments her mother would have with people who thought she was crazy, or those years of dementia at the end of her life, or the times her father had just disappeared, or the nonsense she used to write in her diary.

"Was she kind of like a witch?" asked Nita astutely, making Adela's stomach turn again.

"She wasn't a witch. She was a wonderful person. Very wise," she answered, realizing then that she really did believe that. It was something that had bothered her since she was a child: her mother was so intelligent, but she was always telling Adela absurd stories that made her question her sanity. And of course it wasn't just Adela who didn't understand her mother; people in town felt the same way. In fact, she couldn't remember a time when people didn't look at Ángela like she was crazy. "What's bothering you, Nita?" she asked, trying to understand what was going through her daughter's head and find out what she was up to.

"I think I know what happened to Jaime. I think something took his energy—his life away," she said firmly. "Ama, there's another monster," she continued. She knew her mother wouldn't believe her, but she couldn't lie about something that she knew was real.

"A monster?" asked Adela, thinking that perhaps someone *had* been with Jaime when he got hurt. Maybe someone had caused the accident.

"A horrible, dangerous monster. He took Jaime's life and now I have to get it back for him," answered Nita, though she knew her mother wasn't going to like it.

"There are no monsters," said Adela, looking her in the eye. "I don't know where you're getting these ideas but listen to me"—she moved closer to her daughter and squeezed her hand—"there are no monsters." Then she turned away sadly. "Your grandmother tortured me with stories like that my whole life, and I assure you, there are no monsters." Tears pricked her eyes. Suddenly Nita threw her arms around her.

"I love you, Ama," she said, crying. Adela was confused by her daughter's reaction, but she was grateful for the hug. Nita let go and peered at her mother through her tears. "I wish my grandmother were here," she said sadly. Adela pulled her daughter close for another hug.

José was sitting on a bench, his eyes trained on the town square. He was waiting for Amaya to walk by. Everything that was going on with Nita was making him very nervous. Anttón was just a weak old man, but thanks to him, José's future with Adela and her daughter was up in the air.

He spotted Amaya with her mother, Marta. They were walking hand in hand. José waved and approached them.

"Hello, Marta. Hi, Amaya," he said to the girl, who was looking very sad.

"Hi, José. How is Nita doing?" asked Amaya's mother, concern in her voice.

"She was really upset about the news, but she's feeling a little better now," replied José. "I was actually looking for you, Amaya. I was wondering if you'd stop by to cheer her up. I think it would be good for you both."

A look passed between Marta and Amaya. They had talked about the last few days, about the games the children had been playing and Nita's seemingly endless supply of strange stories. Amaya couldn't see what Nita and Jaime saw, so she didn't understand a lot of the things that had happened. Sometimes she felt frustrated with her friends, but at least the games were always fun.

Nita was flying above the waves crashing against the foot of Mount Jaizkibel, soaring past the rocky points that jutted out like foot soldiers ready to defend the small mountain against an angry sea determined to swallow it whole. This time there was no beast carrying her through the air. It was her against the world. Taking a dizzying turn, she flew into a bank of clouds, where the mist was so thick she could barely see past her nose. Suddenly she found herself in the woods of Mount Ulía. She was alone and on alert, nerves coursing through her battered body.

She turned around and suddenly found herself face to face with the woman in white from her dream. She hadn't known who she was the first time she saw her, but now she knew: it was her grandmother, Ángela. The woman smiled at her. She bent down, bringing her face close to her granddaughter's. Then she reached out and brushed Nita's cheek lovingly. Nita's skin warmed under her touch. Nita tried to speak but no words came out. Ángela took off the bracelet she was wearing and gave it to Nita, who was surprised to find that she wasn't wearing it herself.

Suddenly, Ángela leapt to her feet. The walls of mist surrounding them had begun to shift, revealing the outlines of human figures, coming toward Nita and her grandmother, then moving away, then coming back again. When they got close enough for her to see them, Nita noticed that their faces were blurry. Once in a while their features would become clear, and Nita recognized José, Anttón, Jon the bully and her father among the figures. Nita watched as her grandmother became more and more unnerved by the figures around them. Then four arms reached out and pulled her into the fog. Frightened, Nita ran to help, but suddenly there was no one there, just the mist. She heard something growl behind her. Already on edge from the realization that she was suddenly alone and frightened now by the strange noise, Nita felt a chill run through her body that made the hairs on the back of her neck stand on end. She turned around. An enormous head, similar to Gom's but framed by terrifying tentacles like the ones the nobusk had, emerged from the mist.

Nita woke up with a jolt. She was in her room. She had fallen asleep after her talk with her mother. Her skin was still electrified by the chill she had felt in her dream. She got a pencil and a piece of paper and began to draw her grandmother surrounded by the men with blurry faces. She felt an urgent need to draw what she had seen; it was the same feeling she had had after her first night of adventures. She had always been quite good at drawing, but in the last three days she had spent so much time trying to recall and sketch every last detail of what she had seen that her drawings were becoming very realistic. Her depiction of her grandmother's face was spot-on, and the mysterious men surrounding her also looked much like they had in the dream.

A noise coming from underneath her pillow pulled her away from her drawing. She pounced on the pillow and took the walkie-talkie out from its hiding place. She examined it, checking to see if it was turned on. She waited a few seconds, but it didn't seem to be working. The battery was dead, and Nita didn't have a charger. The noise she had heard must have been the last low battery warning.

There was a knock on her door then and her mother came into her room. Amaya was behind her. Nita jumped out of bed and hugged her friend, who couldn't quite return the hug because she was holding Nita's African masks. Adela left the girls alone and went down to the kitchen to make lunch.

"How are you?" asked Amaya, feeling a little shy around her friend. She felt like she was visiting someone in the hospital.

"I'm OK. My arms hurt, and my stomach too, but I'll be fine," replied Nita as she took the masks from her friend and hung them on the wall.

"I'm glad you're feeling OK," said Amaya. She was surprised, since she had expected Nita to be more upset. That was the impression she had gotten from José, anyway. The girls started to talk about what had happened to Jaime.

"Don't you think that drunk old man had something to do with it?" Amaya asked Nita, sounding convinced.

"No, I talked to him and he told me he didn't do anything," replied Nita after a pause. She wasn't sure how much to say. Maybe it was best to stop involving her friends in this whole mess. After thinking for a moment, she decided that she needed the support of her friend, of someone who believed her. She began to tell the story of what had happened the night before, and Amaya listened, captivated. She told her about the battle with the Nobusk of the East, how it ended, where Jaime was. When she got to that part, Amaya got upset.

"Jaime's in the hospital," she interrupted, her voice stern. Their friend was suffering and she didn't think it was right to make up stories about where he was or what had happened to him.

"I know that. But it's only his body. His spirit is trapped." Nita tried to explain, but she could tell that she was losing Amaya.

"Don't joke about this, Nita. He's in the hospital and he's really sick." Amaya was angry that Nita was still playing this stupid game that she didn't understand instead of dealing with what was happening to their friend in the real world.

"Amaya, I'm not joking. We can help him," she insisted, though she felt her friend slipping away.

"His *doctors* can help him," Amaya corrected her.

The walkie-talkie made another noise. Nita turned her head toward the noise while Amaya, who hadn't heard anything, looked on, bewildered. Nita jumped onto her bed and grabbed the walkie-talkie.

"What are you doing?"

"Shhh!" Nita interrupted, straining to hear something.

"Nita! Can you hear me?" crackled the walkie-talkie.

Nita was astonished. "Yes, I can hear you, Jaime!" she shouted.

"What are you doing?" asked Amaya, confused and uncomfortable.

"Don't you hear it? It's Jaime!" Nita replied, grinning.

"I'm leaving," Amaya said angrily. Her eyes began to water. She had run out of patience for Nita's absurd game, and she suddenly felt very resentful of her friend. Jaime's accident had been hard enough, and now Nita was torturing her for the sake of a stupid game.

"Amaya, please don't make me do this alone," begged Nita with tears in her eyes.

Amaya turned to leave, but then she paused, seeming to reconsider. Then the walkie-talkie crackled again, drawing Nita's attention away from her friend. Amaya left the room crying, and by the time Nita turned around she was gone. Nita clutched her walkie-talkie and stared at the empty doorway, powerless to stop her friend. Her eyes stung with tears.

Adela, who was in the kitchen, saw Amaya run out of the house crying.

"Nita, can you hear me?" crackled Nita's walkie-talkie again, even though the battery was dead.

"Yes, I hear you, Jaime! Where are you?" she answered, her voice shaking. For a few seconds there was only silence.

"I'm somewhere underground . . . there are canons and weapons everywhere," came Jaime's voice.

"Can you get out of there?" she asked, hoping against hope that she could get her best friend back.

"The monster is wounded but I can't get away." The walkie-talkie crackled and cut out. "My body's gone," he continued. Nita could hear the fear in his voice. "Help me."

"I don't know where you are!" shouted Nita, racking her brain to try to figure out where he could be trapped. The walkie-talkie fell silent.

Standing just outside her daughter's door, Adela listened to her daughter's one-sided conversation with a walkie-talkie that wasn't on, her brow furrowed in concern. Nita's voice was the only one she heard. Once again, Nita's behavior made her think of her mother. Her heart ached as she tried to deny something that now seemed undeniable: her little girl was going crazy. She lived for Nita, and she was going to lose her. There wasn't even a crackle from the walkie-talkie, nothing that would explain her daughter's behavior.

Nita crossed the room to her wardrobe and Adela hid behind the door. Suddenly everything was quiet. She couldn't hear Nita moving around anymore. She waited a few seconds before going into the room. Nita wasn't there. It didn't make sense. How could she have left the room when Adela was standing by the door? She looked out the window but she didn't see anyone outside. Then she walked over to the bed, where the drawing Nita had made caught her eye. She picked it up and gasped as she recognized her mother, surrounded by eerie figures. She felt like her world was crumbling around her. *Why? Why is this happening to my baby?* Adela ran out of the house, looking frantically for her daughter. But she was nowhere to be found.

Nita got inside the cabin where she had seen Anttón's dead body the same way she did the first time. She put her key in the lock of her wardrobe and was pulled through the keyhole. She came to a stop in the single room of the small cabin, stopping the inertia that was pulling her forward. She looked around. She was holding Jaime's walkie-talkie.

"Anttón!" she shouted, looking all around for the old man.

There was no answer. She shouted his name a few more times, but the cabin appeared to be empty. Everything was as it had been the last time. The date on the calendar was the same. It made sense: last night Jaime had changed the course of events that would have led to Anttón's death, and it was now one o'clock in the afternoon on the day he would have died. Nita needed to tell someone what she had found out from Jaime. She didn't know how he had been able to contact her but she was certain that the information he had given her was true, and very important. She hoped that Anttón would know what Jaime was talking about. Amaya hadn't believed her. She knew her mother wouldn't even listen to what she had to say. She was unsure about José, but she didn't think he would believe her either. Finding her strange new companions was her only chance to save Jaime. But the cabin was empty.

Something in the corner of the room caught her eye. She hadn't noticed it the last time. There was a small desk there with some oil lamps and candlesticks holding half-melted candles sitting on it. She also saw an inkwell with quills. The tentacle of the Nobusk of the East was propped up against the desk. It had the imprint of Nita's hand on it. She picked it up and grasped it as if it were an exotic sword. It was very light and the edges were sharp. She touched an edge with her finger and winced as the blade cut her. Then she put the tentacle back and continued to examine the desk. There were strange-looking sheets of paper there too. All of them were blank except for one. Nita thought the paper looked very old, or maybe it was just that it was handmade. She tried to read what was written on the single sheet of paper that wasn't blank, but she couldn't understand it. It was written in a language that used letters and pictograms, but she couldn't make sense of it.

There was a small chest of drawers tucked under the desk. Standing on top of it were a number of carved wooden figures that formed a strange little army. Nita looked at them, and when she went to touch one her bracelet began to glow. She turned the figure over in her hands, but she didn't see a keyhole. She opened one of the drawers and saw that it was full of sheets of paper. They looked very old, like the ones on top of the desk, but they were filled with writing on both sides. She grabbed a stack of paper and put it on the desk. She couldn't read any of it. She went to pick up the page on top of the stack and her bracelet brushed the paper.

Suddenly the text started to move. The letters and pictograms peeled off the paper and rearranged themselves in the room, forming animated scenes, like a movie being projected in front of her. She drew her hand back in surprise. Then she touched the bracelet to the text again, and once again the jumble of words and pictures rearranged itself into visual stories that she could understand perfectly. Anttón's voice filled the room. At first he seemed to be speaking a strange language, but then she could understand him. Nita realized that the papers were part of some sort of official report or journal. All the documents featured the same heading: each day's page began with Anttón's voice saying *"The Legacy of the Sap Gatherer"* and a report number. Anttón's voice was clear, and he had no trouble talking. It was as if

Nita were inside his mind, and there he was able to express himself without interruptions.

I saw Adela again today. I think she saw me too, but she pretended she hadn't . . . Things are still quiet. No trace of any danger.

Through Anttón's eyes, Nita watched her mother looking in a store window. The old man followed her with his eyes until she disappeared around a corner.

Nita started to look through the stack of papers and found that she, José and her mother appeared throughout Anttón's journal. She was amazed at the number of times he had been watching her without her realizing it. She gathered the pages and went to put them back in the drawer when the page at the bottom of the stack fell on the floor. When she had grabbed all the pages at once she hadn't gotten a good grip on the bottom one. She knelt down to pick it up and the scene on the page was projected in front of her. Gom and Anttón were battling a group of nobusks on a steep slope. Nita didn't recognize anything about the place. Anttón threw something to the ground, producing a blinding flash of light. When the bright light faded and Nita's eyes had readjusted, she saw Anttón and Gom waking up in the grass near the cabin.

After all the fighting and suffering we finally escaped the temporary prison that our pride and arrogance put us in. The Root has given up. Her plan to destroy us has failed. I don't know if we've won, or if she's just tired of chasing us. My faithful friend Gom is with me.

Through the old man's eyes, Nita saw a woman through the trees. She floated up to the sky and then back down to the ground again as if she were being pulled back and forth by a tide. Then Anttón was watching Nita again. She was playing and laughing happily with her friends.

No one knows what happened to Nita's father. They don't suspect a thing. Adela appears to have moved on. And Ángela . . . who was once so powerful . . . seems to have disappeared. The girl is still so young. She isn't ready. I don't know how long I'll be able to keep Gom under control.

Through Anttón's eyes, Nita watched José leave the house. He appeared relaxed and content. Anttón kept his eyes on him as he walked away. At one point he turned around and looked in Anttón's direction. It was like he knew he was being watched. Anttón hurried to hide behind the corner of a building and lost sight of him.

I'm going to get rid of that impostor.

Nita shivered when she heard those words. Apparently the old man held the key to her father's disappearance. And he wanted to hurt José. José and Nita had a very strong bond. She loved him and had more memories of him than she did of her father. Suddenly the door to the cabin slammed open. Anttón burst into the room, but when he got to his desk there was nobody there. He saw the mess of papers and he knew the little girl had been snooping. His face twisted in anger and he punched the wall hard. The whole cabin shook.

Nita, still clutching her walkie-talkie, appeared in her room. She was at her wit's end. She felt so alone. She didn't have anyone she could trust, no friends or family she could ask for help. How was she going to find Jaime all by herself? Her head was spinning, and at first she didn't notice her mother standing in her room. Adela had heard noises and rushed into the room, desperately hoping that she would find her missing daughter there.

Then Nita looked up and mother and daughter regarded each other wordlessly. Nita was filled with the urge to cry, and Adela with the urge to yell at her daughter once again, to tell her that she wasn't allowed to do whatever it was that she had done. Nita threw herself into her mother's arms, sobbing, unable to say a single word. It was all too much for her. Adela, disarmed, could do nothing but cry along with her daughter. It suddenly dawned on her how much her little girl was suffering. Her anger melted away, and all she felt was compassion and understanding. Maybe her daughter was going crazy, but she had felt the same way once, after Raúl disappeared. And on one of those dark days, a four-year-old Nita had come up to her, playful and giggling, and told her she loved her. Just like that, her daughter had brought her back to reality. Adela had taken comfort in that sweet smile and forged on. Perhaps the little anchor that had once kept her from floating away was fading now, but she wasn't going to spend one more minute dwelling on her doubts or fears. She would fight for her daughter, and she would show her that she would always be by her side.

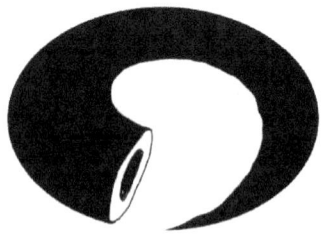

7 THE BATTLE

Nita and Adela got out of the car near the gate to the San Marcos Fort. From where they parked, Adela could see that the gate appeared to be locked. The fort looked deserted. It was built in the late nineteenth century to provide military reinforcement and act as a strategic base in the Carlist Wars that could be used to protect the city of San Sebastián from a possible land or sea attack by the French. It had had different uses through the years, but since 1970 it had only been used for military training exercises. The walls, which were over five feet thick, followed the natural shape of the terrain and camouflaged fairly well with the vegetation on most days, but it was a sunny day and for once they stood out against the landscape. The flat, cold stone that made up the fort was slowly being swallowed by nature: small plants peeked through every crack and hole in the rock and many of the slabs were covered in moss.

After listening calmly to her daughter's bizarre stories, Adela had decided to bring her here. There were other forts in the area, including Txoritokieta and Guadalupe, but something told her to come to San Marcos. She couldn't put it into words, but it was a feeling she had experienced many times throughout her life. She had a feeling something big—good or bad, she didn't know—was going to happen there.

Adela had put together different clues from Nita's stories and arrived at the conclusion that what the little girl was looking for was in this place or a similar one. She had also considered another possibility related to something that had been in the news many times recently: for a moment it had occurred to her that Nita could be describing a cache like the ones the terrorist group ETA used for hiding their weapons and explosives, but it seemed too complicated, even considering the degree of complexity of this whole strange situation. And besides, a weapons cache didn't seem to have anything to do with a little boy, or a giant monster. She had dismissed that idea quickly.

She was having a hard time trying to make sense of Nita's stories. Right now the only thing she could trust was her strange sixth sense; it worried her to follow it like this, but it was radiating from her with such force that she felt that it had to be real. It had taken them a long time to land on San Marcos as the most probable whereabouts of Jaime and the monster that was holding him captive, and it was late afternoon by the time they arrived.

"We have to get inside, Ama!" said Nita, running down the pathway toward the entrance to the fort.

"Wait, Nita!" shouted Adela. When she saw that her daughter wasn't going to stop she slammed the car door shut and ran after her.

Nita had reached a huge, black wrought-iron gate that was chained shut and locked. She rattled the gate in vain. Her mother reached the gate, panting, and saw a bridge on the other side. It was built over a moat, designed to protect the fort from siege, that ran the length of the wall. The bridge led to a path that opened up into a courtyard with a ramp running up to the upper part of the fort. Off the courtyard lay the different parts of the fort, including the barracks, store rooms for supplies and food, the armory and a cistern for water. The fort was designed to sustain two hundred men during a siege for one hundred and forty-three days with no supplies from the outside.

"We can't get in," said Adela.

They looked through the bars but they couldn't make anything out on the other side. Suddenly a shadow moved on the edge of their vision. Mother and daughter jumped back.

"Jaime!" shouted Nita desperately.

"We can't get through the gate, Nita. I think we should call the police," said Adela, trying to calm her daughter down. But they would have to find a phone first, and they were very far from any telephones. Nita regarded her mother nervously. She knew what to do, but she didn't know how her mother would react. They couldn't turn back now. There was obviously something in that fort. They had to keep going.

"Ama, come over here," said Nita, taking her mother's arm with her left hand and fitting the charm on her bracelet into the lock on the gate with her right hand.

"What—?" began Adela, but she didn't finish her thought. Suddenly her feet dropped out from under her as she and her daughter teleported through the gate guarding the entrance to the fort. They came to a stop and Adela doubled over, trying to understand what had just happened while simultaneously struggling to keep her lunch down. Nita looked at her, fear and uncertainty written across her face. She was worried that her mother would be angry with her and she would be on her own again. She wouldn't know what to do. Just then they heard a noise. It was coming from the courtyard. Nita ran to investigate, leaving her mother there to recover. Adela tried to say something but she couldn't get a single word out. Clutching her stomach, she ran after her daughter.

It looked like the coast was clear. A small well used with the cistern was the only thing that stood out in the courtyard, which was covered in solid paving stones. There were archways carved in the stone wall lining the courtyard and under the steep ramp that led to the upper part of the fort. Each archway framed a closed wooden door.

"What just happened?" Adela asked her daughter,

struggling to understand. Nita looked at her, her face serious. "What happened back there? What did you do?" she asked again as the reality of the situation began to set in.

"I told you, Ama, this bracelet is magic," Nita replied. She didn't know what to say to her mother. All she had was this simple explanation. If there was someone who held the answers to her mother's questions, that person wasn't there at the moment. And the extent of the powers of the strange bracelet was anyone's guess.

"We went through the gate and . . . and now we're inside," said Adela, looking around nervously. "This is military property. There's something—dangerous—here," she whispered, fearful of the real danger of trespassing as well as the feeling she had that there was some other threat lurking. Many of the most important events in her life had been preceded by strange feelings, but she had never recognized their significance because she had failed to make the connection between the feeling and the event. She had never wanted to give credit to those feelings because doing so would mean recognizing the truth behind certain stories she simply couldn't let herself believe, which had been the source of some of her worst fights with her mother. She could recall many tense moments in their relationship in which they both held on stubbornly to their arguments, neither one allowing herself to be convinced by the other. Now she was beginning to suspect that she had been in the wrong.

Nita approached an archway. The doors were made of thick wood and had small windows at the height of an adult's head. Nita grabbed the frame and jumped up to look through the window, but she couldn't see anything inside. There was barely any light: it would make the perfect hiding place for a dark creature like the Nobusk of the East. Adela went to another door and was peering through the window when something banged on the door from the inside, making the wood rattle. Adela and Nita backed away from the doors and into the sunlight that still bathed the courtyard. Something banged on the door again, hard. Nita remembered the monster from the night before and suddenly wished that Gom were with them. But she couldn't trust him or the old man. Theoretically the nobusk was smaller in the daylight, and she thought she might be able to defeat it with the help of her bracelet. But she didn't know how to get Jaime out from inside the monster. The banging was so loud that Adela and Nita didn't notice that Anttón and Gom had appeared behind them.

"You shouldn't have come here," said Gom, startling Nita. He was standing next to Anttón, who was holding a sledgehammer.

Nita spun around, frightened, and ran to her mother's side. Adela turned to see what had scared her daughter and jumped when she saw Anttón. She couldn't see Gom. Nita's stories had seemed so far-fetched, but here was yet another piece of evidence to back them up.

"What are you doing here?" she asked the old man.

"You don't know what you're dealing with," answered Anttón, struggling to get the words out.

"You know what happened to my father and now you want to hurt José," Nita accused Anttón.

"You're wrong, little one," said Gom, as Anttón shook his head.

"I saw it in the papers on his desk. And you're his friend," she reproached Gom. Adela watched her daughter talking to thin air.

"Who are you talking to?" she asked, concern in her voice. Nita looked at her, puzzled. After everything she had told her and everything that had happened she couldn't believe that her mother couldn't see the enormous creature standing in front of them. Amaya hadn't been able to see him either.

"Why can't you see him?" she asked, bewildered.

"She has to believe in you, in your words. Her mind is refusing to acknowledge my existence," answered Gom.

Nita's eyes filled with tears. "Ama, why don't you believe me?" Adela refused to accept that Nita's stories were true. If she did, it would mean that her mother had been telling the truth all along, and that she had failed her by not believing her. And it would mean that all those hard decisions she had made for the good of her mother, her wonderful mother, had been horribly wrong. But Nita was sobbing, and watching her daughter suffer made her heart ache.

"I don't see anything," she said sadly.

Anttón put the sledgehammer down then and slowly approached Adela, who didn't flinch. The old man put his arms around her and clutched her tight. Nita looked on in shock. She stopped crying abruptly.

"My love, my life," Anttón whispered in Adela's ear. He didn't stutter.

Now it was Adela's turn to cry. "Who *are* you?" she asked, pulling away so that she could see the old man's face. "It can't be . . . this is impossible," she stammered.

Anttón nodded, his face serious. "It's me," he said, once again without stuttering. It was as if he had been practicing those words for so long that the physical and mental barrier that normally kept him from speaking clearly wasn't strong enough to hold them back. Adela, still in disbelief, looked at her daughter.

"What's going on?" Nita asked her, worry written on her face.

"It's impossible . . ." said Adela, sounding dazed. "The only person who ever called me that was your—" Suddenly Anttón picked up the sledgehammer and lunged toward them, his face twisted in rage.

Just when it looked like Anttón was going to attack Adela and Nita, he ran between the mother and daughter and brought the sledgehammer down hard on the Nobusk of the East. The shadows had been slowly creeping into the courtyard, and the dark creature had been forced out of his hiding place. He was still weak from the battle with Nita and they had him cornered.

Anttón's attack brought Adela out of her state of shock. When the sledgehammer connected with the terrible monster, it gave off a shock wave that revealed part of his body to Adela. It disappeared momentarily and then reappeared when Anttón struck another blow. Finally Adela saw the creature's whole body, although it was reduced in size because there was still some sunlight. But the light was disappearing by the minute, and with it, their strategic advantage.

Adela had slowly been backing away from the monster in fear. She was heading right for Gom, but her back was turned toward him so she didn't notice. Gom, meanwhile, was watching the battle intently. "The sun is going down," he said, looking at the edge of the shadows. "He's growing stronger by the minute," he said nervously.

Adela turned at the sound of his voice and was so startled that she lost her balance and fell. She scrambled to her feet and ran to her daughter, shielding her with her body. "It's a dragon! Don't come near us, monster!" she said to Gom.

"I'm not a dragon. What exactly would you do to me anyway?" he asked, slowly moving toward the protective mother. Adela didn't know what to say. She was frozen with fear. Gom continued to move toward Adela and Nita, picking up speed. When he was inches away he jumped over them and threw himself on the nobusk. Just then the nobusk landed a blow that sent Anttón flying. He landed a few feet in front of Adela and Nita. Adela ran to his aid. The old man was bruised, but it didn't take him long to get up. He gestured to Adela that he was fine. Then he bent down in front of Nita.

"I'll help you save him," he said.

Nita looked at her mother in silence. Neither of them knew what to do. Adela couldn't believe it, but the stories Nita had told her were true. There really was a monster, and Anttón, a complete stranger, was actually . . . the love of her life. She knew what to do then.

"*Txiki*, I am so sorry I didn't believe you," she said with tears in her eyes. They were the tears she hadn't shed for her mother, tears of sadness, of frustration with her own ignorance, her blindness. "If we want to have any chance of saving Jaime, we've got to do something now," she said firmly, even though she had no idea what they were up against and she had a very uncomfortable feeling that was telling her that this was going to end badly, but at the same time that there was no other way.

"I have to get him out of there," said Nita.

Anttón, his face serious, looked first at Adela and then at Nita. "Gr-grab . . ." he began, but then he gave up and showed her what to do instead: he took hold of Nita's hand and pulled hard. Nita understood what she had to do. It would be very risky. Together, they ran toward Gom, who had the nobusk cornered. Once in a while Jaime's hand and face could be seen inside the creature's belly.

"I see him!" shouted Nita, pointing at the nobusk. Without hesitating, she ran to the wounded beast, who was trapped against the stone column between two of the archways in the passage. Fear had made the beast very nervous, and when Nita approached, he immediately lunged at her.

"Look out!" shouted Gom, throwing himself between the nobusk and the girl. The resulting collision of the two beasts sent Gom barreling back toward Nita. Nita saw him coming and dove to the side, narrowly avoiding being crushed. The nobusk changed targets then, charging at Anttón. The old man was able to grab his sledgehammer again and deliver two powerful blows to the beast. The nobusk reacted by grasping Anttón in his claws and launching himself up to the top level of the fort.

"No!" shouted Adela, surprising herself with her reaction to what she was seeing. She felt like her reason to live was being taken from her all over again. Nita looked at her mother in surprise and then turned her eyes to follow the nobusk and the old man up until they disappeared from view. She scrambled to her feet and climbed on top of Gom, using the chains on his body to clamber up to his shoulder. Gom took off silently toward the top of the fort. Adela nervously watched them disappear. Then she looked for a way to reach them, finally setting off up the ramp that led to the top level.

Now on the upper level of the fort, Anttón used the sledgehammer to escape the nobusk's grasp. The sun was sinking, but the final rays of light weakened the son of shadows and mud. Anttón wielded the sledgehammer masterfully, knocking back every tentacle his adversary sent his way. The nobusk whimpered with each blow. Gom and Nita reached the top of the fort, landing like a bomb on top of the nobusk. Together, Gom and Anttón were able to subdue the nobusk.

"Now, little one! It's time!" shouted Gom as he struggled to control multiple tentacles. Nita jumped from his shoulder, landing on top of the nobusk, and when she saw a hand push up against the black skin of the beast she grabbed it with her right hand and pulled as hard as she could. The nobusk writhed in pain as if its insides were being torn out. Planting her feet on the nobusk's body and pulling as hard as an eleven-year-old girl could, after a number of attempts Nita was finally able to wrench a ghost-like Jaime from inside the beast. He looked like a spirit from one of the scary stories she had read at school. Jaime floated above Nita, his face only inches away from hers. There were dark particles floating in the air around this strange ghost-Jaime. His face was different; there was something unnatural about it. His eyes had turned black, as black as night. Then he smiled, but it was a strange smile: it looked more like an evil grin. Suddenly, he whooshed away from the fort. The nobusk stopped writhing and lay still on the ground.

Adela was rushing up the ramp to the top level of the fort when Jaime's life floated by her. He glanced at her, curious, before continuing on his way out of the fort. Interestingly, he didn't fly into the air, floating up into the clouds. Instead, he hovered only a few feet above the ground. Adela had to move aside to avoid running into him.

Panting, she finally arrived at the top of the fort and ran to Nita, who was flanked by Anttón and Gom. She still hadn't gotten used to the sight of that incredible beast. "Nita, are you all right?" she shouted, praying that her daughter was unharmed. Her voice shook with fear.

"Ama, did you see the monster? We did it!" Nita shouted excitedly.

"What the hell is going on, Anttón?" asked Adela, turning to the old man. Gom turned to face her. Adela balked at the size of the beast. "I don't understand what's happening. I feel like I'm going to go crazy if I don't get some answers."

"You won't like the answers," warned Gom.

"Ama, I already told you about the Root—"

"I'm not talking about the Root, little one," interrupted the huge beast, leaning down to bring his face close to Nita's. Nita looked from Gom to Anttón to her mother in confusion.

"Where have you been this whole time?" Adela asked the old man.

"Fighting," Anttón growled with difficulty.

"We've been fighting that terrible monster, the Root, for fifty years. But in your time, those years were only months," explained Gom.

"Great, yet another story that doesn't make sense!" shouted Adela in frustration.

"I saw you fighting the Root!" shouted Nita, remembering the scene from the papers she had found in Anttón's cabin and the woman who had moved with such ease in the air. Nita could still see her jumping high into the sky and then plunging back down to the ground again, moving between the earth and the sky as if it were all one big swimming pool, all at an incredible speed. "I saw it in the papers I found in the cabin."

Adela listened to her daughter and then fixed her eyes on Anttón. "But you're so different. Your voice, your face . . ." she said sadly.

Anttón approached her and looked deep into her eyes. "It's me," he said, his eyes filling with tears. Adela couldn't make sense of any of it, but something inside her told her that the old man was telling the truth. Suddenly, her anguish and longing melted away. She had found what she had spent the last five years searching for. With a sob, she threw her arms around the old man in front of her.

"I don't understand, Ama. Who is he, my grandfather?" asked a very confused but enthralled Nita, who had slowly moved closer and was now standing at her mother's side.

Anttón turned, knelt down and enveloped her in a huge hug. Nita looked up at her mother, whose eyes were brimming with tears. "He's your father, Raúl," she said. Nita was stunned speechless. Her heart began to beat very fast, so fast she felt like it could burst.

"The very same instrument that had helped us in our fight was our perdition in the end. The bracelet you're wearing belongs to you and only you. No one else can use it. We tried to use it, and we got trapped," explained the huge beast, his voice tired. "Ángela lost her mind in the battle and Anttón and I were consigned to oblivion."

Night fell on the small fort, enveloping the newly reunited family in a blanket of darkness. They were so wrapped up in the moment that they were oblivious to any danger. Gom was the first to notice that something wasn't right.

"I don't like this at all," he said, sniffing the air.

He turned to look at the spot where the Nobusk of the East lay and watched in horror as two other nobusks emerged from the shadows.

"Ranku, the Nobusk of the South," he growled, looking toward the creature now standing to the left of the nobusk they had defeated. "And Ranku-Gor, his most despicable follower," he finished, gesturing toward the monster on the creature's right flank. The two nobusks, drawing strength from the darkness of the night, were full size. A single nobusk had brought Gom and Anttón, two seasoned soldiers, close to defeat; a fight with two of the beasts would almost certainly end in tragedy. Anttón stood up, his tired body tight with tension, and, grasping his sledgehammer, walked toward the three nobusks. He stopped when he reached Gom.

"Take your friend and be on your way!" shouted Gom. The two nobusks picked up their fallen comrade and, watching Anttón and Gom suspiciously, slunk away. The two soldiers were visibly relieved. Anttón turned and ran toward Adela and Nita.

"We have to—" he began with difficulty.

"We have to leave this place!" Gom interrupted, finishing

his thought for him. The two old friends knew why the other two nobusks had come. They were there to help their comrade, and that meant helping him complete his mission. The three deadly assassins all had the same objective: to destroy Anttón, and anyone around him.

Suddenly one of the nobusks flew out of the shadows, throwing himself on Gom. The two beasts began to fight, moving in a tangle across the top level of the fort. The other nobusk emerged from the shadows behind Nita and Adela, but Anttón reached them first. He had just managed to grab Nita when the nobusk landed a terrible blow that sent the old man and the girl flying in the air toward the opening in the top of the fort, below which lay the inner courtyard. Anttón held the girl as they plummeted toward the hard stone floor, positioning himself so that his body would protect her from the impact. A huge mouth grabbed Adela by the neck. All she could do was watch them fall.

Nita and Anttón hit the ground hard. Anttón's chest broke the girl's fall, but she was thrown off of him by the force of the impact. Anttón lay motionless on the ground. Nita, her back toward Anttón, picked herself up gingerly. Wearily, she turned around. When she saw Anttón sprawled on the ground she ran to his side.

"Anttón, Anttón!" she shouted. The old man didn't move. A puddle of blood was forming under his head.

"My daughter . . ." His voice was weak but he didn't stutter. He could see everything clearly now. He knew he was dying, but he was suddenly flooded with an incredible sense of peace.

"Anttón, please tell me you're okay!" Nita cried.

"My daughter . . . listen to me," he gasped. "You have to come find me . . . use the bracelet." Nita looked at him through her tears. She didn't know what to say. "Do you hear me? My little girl," he said, bringing his hand up to touch her face. A loud growl came from the top level of the fort and Gom crashed to the ground next to them. Stunned by the fall, he lay still. "Nita, you have great power. Take care of your mother . . . now go," he whispered, his strength leaving him.

The old man relaxed completely, his eyes staring. Nita sobbed and shook her head. She couldn't believe this was happening. Her father had died in front of her. Adela screamed from the top of the fort, bringing Nita to her senses. She looked over at Gom, who was struggling to get up, and then at her bracelet. Then she scrambled to her feet. She had a plan. Maybe it was naive or suicidal or both, but she was going to go through with it, no matter what the consequences.

Adela was in the air, trapped in the jaws of one of the nobusk's many mouths. Suddenly the beast opened its mouth and she fell to the ground, landing on her knees. Panting from exertion and fear, she began to stand up, but then the nobusk struck again. A tentacle pierced her in the gut. The beast began to use its tentacle to pump the life out of Adela's body. Her energy was slowly draining out of her, but she was unable to move. Her eyes turned white.

But the dark beast's plan was cut short. Suddenly the nobusk was watching his tentacle fly through the air, sliced off with a weapon that had cut so cleanly that it had to be incredibly sharp. Frantically he looked around for the culprit and found that the weapon had been wielded by a miniscule and apparently harmless creature. It was Nita. It had taken her ten seconds to teleport to the cabin, grab the crystallized tentacle of the Nobusk of the East and reappear in the thick of the battle.

Adela fell to the ground, panting but alive. Nita charged at the nobusk, swinging her strange sword in the air as the huge beast dodged her attacks. The nobusk hit her with one of his tentacles, sending her flying backwards. Nita did a somersault in the air and landed on her feet, touching the tip of her sword to the ground to balance herself. Her expression was clouded. She was entirely focused on her enemy. She rushed toward her target at an impossible speed, faster than she had ever run, faster than *anyone* had ever run. When she reached the nobusk she brought her sword down in a huge arc that cut through the beast's side. A black liquid poured from the wound and onto the ground, but it sunk into the earth just as its tentacle had. The nobusk was turning to face Nita when his comrade appeared, lunging at the girl. The beast never made contact with his target, as Gom dealt him a blow that sent him soaring high into the air. The other nobusk used the distraction to make his escape.

"Don't let your guard down! They may attack again!" the gomulus said to Nita. They both looked around. "They never leave without completing their mission!" he finished, his body showing the tension they both felt as they waited for the nobusks to come back. Nita turned her gaze to her mother and felt a rush of surprise and relief when she saw that she was getting up. She ran to her. As soon as she reached Adela, mother and daughter threw their arms around each other. Nita burst into tears.

Gom looked on, finally allowing himself to relax as the realization came that the nobusks had already fulfilled their mission. They were no longer in danger; the Root's assassins had killed one of the worthiest enemies she had faced in centuries. The tired old gatherer had died doing his duty, protecting his sap, and his life had burned out before their eyes. The huge beast hung his head as sorrow overcame him. His comrade in arms was gone.

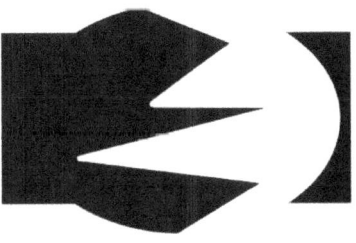

8 A NEW LIFE

It was very early on a sunny day in August, and all was quiet and calm in the mountains. Some patches of early-morning fog still lingered in the woods, making the air humid and slightly stifling. José was climbing up Peñas de Aia by himself, a small backpack slung over his shoulder, while Gom and Nita were sitting in silence on the peak of another nearby mountain, Urdaburu, resting and thinking. Nita was close enough to José for him not to worry, but far enough away to enjoy a bit of privacy and quiet.

Recent events had caused quite a commotion in town. The body of an eighty-year-old man had been found at San Marcos Fort. He had fallen from the top of the fort. A police investigation had yielded no answers, and the case was filed as unsolved; no one came close to imagining the real story behind what had happened, of course.

Jaime's mother had jumped out of her chair when all the

machines her little boy was hooked up to suddenly fried in a spectacular fireworks show of sparks. When she recovered from the surprise she looked down to see that her son was awake. He felt freezing cold when she pulled him into a hug. She didn't notice the strange expression in his eyes. There was no way she could have known that the life inside his body had changed irreparably. The family was overjoyed at his apparent recovery.

Adela's energy seemed to have abandoned her. The strange creature she had encountered a few days before had taken part of her life. Everyone could tell there was something wrong, but it made sense, given everything she had been through in recent years. "A textbook case of depression," one of the town gossips had called it. In some ways she was better off than before, since she was no longer searching for Raúl, but once again the love of her life had slipped through her fingers like some precious liquid no container could hold.

José sat down on a fallen tree trunk in a wooded area and took out a water bottle. A thin root snaked up behind him and, with a sharp movement, thrust itself into his left ear. He sat straight up, his body going taut like a piano wire. The trunk of the tree in front of him took on the shape of a woman's face.

"You're the one who summoned the Nobusk of the East," said a woman's voice inside José's head.

"Yes," choked out José.

"A mere gatherer may not summon a nobusk."

"I wanted to give you your enemy's head as proof of my loyalty."

"Well things didn't go as planned, did they? Two of my best soldiers are near death," hissed the voice, and the root snaked further into José's brain. The man's face screwed up in pain.

"Argh," he grunted. "But the old man's dead. He had to be taken care of."

"I know what you want. I am inside your mind. But you have let loose a force whose power is unknown to all of us. You must keep it under control until I arrive."

"Y-y-yes, I have a plan."

"Yes, the boy could be useful. If he cannot be turned he must be eliminated. The girl is too powerful."

"Yes, but I'll make sure she doesn't get any stronger, and anyway, there's another—"

"Another girl," the Root interrupted. A grin of satisfaction spread across the face in the tree.

Amaya was looking out her bedroom window, feeling sad about losing her friend. Nita had betrayed her. She had let her down. Amaya kept a picture from a fishing trip the three friends had taken the summer before in her nightstand. She took it out and looked at it sadly. She couldn't wait to see Jaime and talk to him again. But thinking about Nita gave her a strange, unpleasant feeling.

Nita and Gom were looking at the horizon, calm and relaxed. Nita was thinking about her father, about how little she knew about him, about his last words: "Come find me." Where was she supposed to look? She had only known him for three days, and she had been so stupid: half of those days she had been running from him or trying to kill him. All she had wanted from that summer was to spend all day playing with her friends and go to the dance at the town's summer festival, but instead she had dived head first into the cruel world of adults. She would always look back on that summer as the beginning of her new life, which would be spent solving mysteries and finding answers about her past, her present and her future. In her hands she held a drawing of the silhouette of a woman, surrounded by trees. She had seen her in one of her father's strange journal entries. Her only option, as terrifying as it was, was to find that woman and get some answers. The innocent games of her childhood were a thing of the past now.

Gom looked over at the girl and saw in her face the features of the man who had fought alongside him for the past fifty years. She had great potential, he could tell: without anyone asking her to, she had taken on some of the most powerful beasts on the planet. She still had a lot to learn, but she might be their only hope for defeating the Root. She was still very young, of course. Who knew what the future held for her? There were so many questions that had yet to be answered. But there was one thing he was sure of.

He turned to Nita, who was still absorbed in her drawing. "I'm hungry," he said. The girl looked at him and grinned.

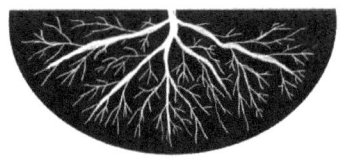

ABOUT THE AUTHOR

Hi. I hope you enjoyed reading this fantasy story set in the time when I grew up. My aim was to keep you entertained for a couple of hours by bringing you into a recognizable world with an element of fantasy. This story is the first chapter in the *Nita's Treasure* series. I hope to publish it in short installments like the one you hold in your hands. My background is in writing screenplays for short and feature-length animated films. I've tried to tell this story in a way that pulls readers into the action by presenting the plot without too many frills, allowing me to maintain a fast pace from the beginning to the end. My experience in film will have a big presence in the stories I'll be telling you.

For more information, check out the website.

www.eltesorodenita.es

To get in touch: info@eltesorodenita.es

www.ingramcontent.com/pod-product-compliance
Lightning Source LLC
Chambersburg PA
CBHW070502130626
46555CB00003B/1124